"Come to Spain with me."

The invitation is husky, his voice deep and accented. I blink, not understanding. His finger inches lower, toward my lips. I have to swallow back a groan. "I can't."

"Come to see my casino there. You cannot truly form an opinion on the merits of my proposal until you have witnessed one for yourself."

"I know enough."

He's surprised by my rapid shift, but surprise quickly morphs into determination. "Are you afraid to be proved wrong?"

"There's no chance of that. I'll never approve of gambling."

"Casinos are so much more than gambling," he says dismissively. He closes the distance between us. "Come to Spain and see for yourself."

My heart twists, my ability to think clearly impeded once more.

"Or are you afraid of what will happen once you leave this gilded cage?"

Clare Connelly was raised in small-town Australia among a family of avid readers. She spent much of her childhood up a tree, Harlequin book in hand. Clare is married to her own real-life hero, and they live in a bungalow near the sea with their two children. She is frequently found staring into space—a surefire sign she is in the world of her characters. She has a penchant for French food and ice-cold champagne, and Harlequin novels continue to be her favorite-ever books. Writing for Harlequin Presents is a long-held dream. Clare can be contacted via clareconnelly.com or on her Facebook page.

Clare Connelly

———

MY FORBIDDEN ROYAL FLING

HARLEQUIN
PRESENTS

HARLEQUIN®
PRESENTS®

Recycling programs
for this product may
not exist in your area.

ISBN-13: 978-1-335-56880-9

My Forbidden Royal Fling

This edition published by arrangement with Harlequin Books S.A.

For questions and comments about the quality of this book,
please contact us at CustomerService@Harlequin.com.

Harlequin Enterprises ULC
22 Adelaide St. West, 40th Floor
Toronto, Ontario M5H 4E3, Canada
www.Harlequin.com

Printed in U.S.A.

MY FORBIDDEN
ROYAL FLING

For Dan, whom I've known and loved more than half my life.

PROLOGUE

Ménage à Billionaire!

THE HEADLINE SCREAMS at me, right above the way-too-handsome face of Santiago del Almodovár, his eyes looking directly at the camera lens, so it feels as though he's staring right through me. And, even though we're separated by several countries, a shiver runs the length of my spine, a rush of apprehension. He's flanked on either side by beautiful women, one blonde, one with cherry-red hair, different in looks but no doubt interchangeable to a man like Santiago. Derision curls my lips.

'This is seriously the man you wish to get involved with?' I can't help but sniff as I address my country's Prime Minister, a man I've always thought had good judgement.

'I understand his reputation isn't particularly savoury, Your Highness...' An embarrassed laugh comes through the phone line. 'But he's well-funded and his investment has the support of the entire parliament.'

'His reputation isn't just unsavoury, Prime Minister, it's disgraceful. From my admittedly brief research, there's nothing to recommend this man except the fact he's "well-funded",' I say quietly, buying time. *His investment has the support of the entire parliament* is a sentence that speaks volumes.

I take it as the gentle warning the minister intends. This is a *fait accompli*. While technically my approval is required to sign off on the deal, I'd be going against my parliament and decades of legal precedent if I refuse. But how the hell can I let this happen? What would my parents think? That's easy. They might have died many years ago—too many—but I hear my father's voice loud and clear, his disapproval, his sadness. This is the exact opposite of what he'd want, and I swore I'd always follow in his footsteps.

I drop my head forward, catching it in the palm of my free hand, the other hand tightening my grip on the phone.

'He's offering a king's ransom for the land.'

Bleakness washes through me. There is no King now, no Queen either. There's just me, a princess, desperately trying to stave off financial ruin for the kingdom without sacrificing the culture of my people, doing everything I can to do justice to my title as my parents would have expected.

'At what price, though?' I murmur, sitting straighter, staring straight ahead. A tapestry hangs on the wall across from me, an ancient piece that I loved even as a little girl.

Out of nowhere, I hear my father's voice. *You must remember, we are Marlsdovens and, while the world knocks at our door, we must answer without being trampled. What makes us unique has to be protected at all costs.*

'My assistant will send through the contracts, Your Highness. If you could sign them—'

'I shall look at them and get back to you,' I interrupt. I hate the idea of a man like that owning such a prime piece of the city's real estate, and I loathe his plans for the site—a glitzy, gaudy casino that will turn our ancient, cultural principality into the exact opposite of my father's vision.

I'm a caretaker for this country—the throne is mine temporarily—and my duty is to look after the people as best I can. What would my father say if he knew I was allowing this to happen? *Make it worth it.* I hear his advice as surely as if he'd breathed the words into the room. Sitting straighter, I grip the phone in my hands.

'Prime Minister?'

'Yes, Your Highness?'

'I'd like to meet with him.' *Make it worth it.* What if I can get him to agree to terms that will truly make this idea worthwhile? And, if he doesn't like my suggestion, then he can simply walk away. After all, he obviously wants the land badly, so why not barter with him, ensure the deal is as advantageous as it can possibly be?

'There's no need for that.' He's scandalised by the very idea, and I can understand why. Santiago's reputation precedes him by about three thousand football fields. He's a lothario through and through, a man as famous for his hard-core partying lifestyle as for the multiple women he wines, dines, beds then moves on from.

'Are you worried I won't be able to handle him, sir?'

The Prime Minister sighs. 'He is a fierce negotiator.'

'I'll cope,' I murmur crisply, my eyes straying to the screen. 'Please arrange it as soon as possible. Thank you.'

It's only a still photo, but his eyes seem to be mocking, taunting… I shut the lid and scrape back my chair. If Santiago wants to buy this land, he can jump through a few hoops first— and, if he's not willing to do that, he can go to hell.

CHAPTER ONE

THE SUNLIGHT BATHES the palace courtyard in a pale glow. It's dappled by the surrounding birch trees so it forms a lattice effect on the ground, and across the man striding towards me.

I've been braced for this—him—for days. The security report on the Spanish tycoon was extensive and detailed—at my request. It confirmed much of what my own searching had done. He lives fast, loose, reckless, with little care for his reputation, his health or, so far as I can tell, for anyone in his orbit. Santiago del Almodovár is the kind of man I loathe.

His stride is long, courtesy of his height—easily six and a half feet—so he comes towards me too quickly. He stares at me with eyes that are a rich, pale brown, almost golden like a wolf's, enigmatic and intense, as though he can see right through me.

I paste an ice-cold smile on my face, tight and distinctly warning. He's wearing a suit—sort of. Navy trousers, a white shirt and a blazer, the shirt unbuttoned at the neck and no tie. It's a strikingly casual look for a guest here at Sölla Palace, but the security council included a note to say that Santiago has very little regard for established conventions. Privately I wonder if it's not a tool he uses to wrong-foot people from the first meeting and thus gain a hint of advantage in negotiations.

As he draws close, I wait for the trademark bow my rank generally commands. He stops two feet short of me, his own smile mocking in a way that stirs butterflies inside me to a fever pitch. His eyes probe mine and a shiver comes out of nowhere. I suppress it, ignoring his lack of protocol, extending my hand in a universal gesture.

'Mr del Almodóvar, thank you for coming.'

'Princess…'

He fills my title with a husky accent, warm and spiced, like the Barcelona sun that fed his soul as a child. Another shiver threatens my equilibrium, but it's quickly overtaken by lightning as he curves his far larger hand around mine, confident and firm, his touch sending a thousand volts of electricity from my fingertips to my arm and then through my entire body. It takes every ounce of self-possession to conceal my reaction, but I pull my hand away as quickly as I can, flexing my fingers at my side.

'Please.' I gesture to the steps, swallowing to cover the hoarseness in my voice. My breath is strained and inwardly I groan. Why, of all people, at all times, do I need to develop a sudden awareness of Santiago del Almodóvar's sex appeal? I'm twenty-four and I've never so much as kissed a man—it's not easy to date when you're the only surviving member of the Marlsdoven royal family. I've never met anyone that's tempted me before, either.

Perhaps it's also the knowledge that my parents have chosen my husband for me, my eventual marriage arranged before I was born. Their dearest wish had been for their daughter to wed the youngest son of their closest friends. I found out shortly after they died; perhaps that's what prevented me from getting involved with anyone. I've literally never had my head turned. I mean, I can tell when someone is objectively handsome or charming, and I enjoy spending time with nice, interesting people, but I've never met a guy and felt anything like a spark.

Why this man?

Why now?

I clamp my teeth together, reminding myself of all the reasons I need to focus. His desire to buy valuable crown land and place a casino on the riverbanks of this ancient, proud city is a threat to everything I hold dear. I have to control this.

'Nice palace,' he murmurs as we step inside the enormous golden doors, each flanked by a guard dressed in full ceremonial uniform. He pays the compliment without it sounding remotely genuine. It's a joke, if anything. I draw my brows together, surprised, because most guests to Sölla are so overwhelmed by the thousand-year-old rooms and the grandiose fittings that I have to work overtime to put them at ease before we can achieve any sensible conversation. But this man has vast personal wealth, earning more in a year than my country's GDP; I gather he's not easily impressed.

That sharpens something inside me, a curl of derision. Because wealth and luxury are one thing, but history quite another. Anyone who can stand inside this grand hall—with its ornate stone carvings made by the hands of men who lived eleven hundred years ago, its vaulted ceilings breathtakingly high, its stained-glass windows perfectly capturing the afternoon sunlight—and be immune to its beauty must surely be a philistine of the highest order.

And? What more can I expect from a man who's made his fortune by building casinos where people go to lose their livelihoods and all hope? People like my uncle, whose addiction cost him so much, ultimately his life. The thought cuts through me, and for a second I'm almost swallowed by nauseating panic. My parents hated gambling. The idea of a casino here in Marlsdoven was absolutely forbidden. What would my dad have said?

Since my parents died, all I've wanted is to make them proud, to make the decisions they'd expect me to make. Dad would have known how to get out of this; he'd have known how to dissuade the Prime Minister. I have never wished for my parents to be here more than I do now.

I squeeze my eyes shut as we walk, sucking in a shaking breath that doesn't quite reach my lungs. Stars dance against my eyelids. I see my parents and their disappointment and feel a horrible sense of failure wash over me.

Santiago makes no attempt at small talk as I lead him through the grand hall and into a narrow but no less impressive corridor—this one flanked by portraits of the royal family going back hundreds of years. My eyes stray to my parents as I pass and my heart lurches with the constant ache I feel for them even now, seven years after their shocking deaths. I can't meet my dad's eyes. I know he'd hate this; my resolution to honour their memory is in tatters.

A state room has been prepared for our meeting, but I realise the error of that as we enter, for the room is not large, and in here Santiago's presence is overwhelming. My pulse goes into overdrive as I turn to face him, so much more aware of him now. Not only is he tall but broad too, like a warrior pretending to be a businessman. I have the sense that he could tame a lion with his bare hands. I don't know where the idea comes from but it's deeply disturbing, on many levels, so I push it aside. I'd seen dozens of photos of him by now, so I'd known he was handsome, but I hadn't been expecting the effects of that in person.

Because he's not just 'handsome'. In reality, there are nuances that the cameras hadn't properly highlighted—a scar at the top of his lip that gives it a slightly angular shape, for example; and a smattering of freckles across the bridge of his nose. They're barely visible because of his dark tan, but they're there, and there's something about them that is wild, fascinating and dangerously distracting. His hair is thick and dark, with a slight curl where it's longer at the nape, and as I stare at him he lifts a hand and runs it through his hair, watching me with those lupine eyes until my stomach is in knots.

'He will seek to gain the advantage any way he can,' my closest aide, Claudia, had advised, her own preparation equal to my own. 'Be on guard.'

The memory of her words is timely. A palace staffer appears at the door and I relax, the sight of a familiar uniform and face reminding me who and where I am. This is my turf, my palace, my people, and he wants something from me: my land.

'Your Highness.' The staff member curtseys, earning another derisive half-smile from the Spanish billionaire. I grind my teeth, an inexplicable urge to somehow knock that infuriating look from his face making my palms hot. 'Are you ready for afternoon tea?'

I turn to my guest, a *frisson* of heat running through me. 'Mr del Almodóvar, would you like something to eat or drink?'

'A beer,' he says without skipping a beat.

I pivot to the maid. 'A beer for our guest and tea for me, thank you.'

I can't shake the feeling he's laughing at me, so I experience a sense of pique as I gesture to the two armchairs set opposite one another in front of a floor-to-ceiling window that frames a stunning view of the Laltussen river. Usually, the river gives me calm. It is ancient and courageous, undaunted by time and man's impulses.' It is a constant in the lives of my people and I take solace from that when I look out on it. But today I am apparently not able to be calmed.

When he sits, it's exactly as you might expect––no hint of reserve or respect for the ancient room and its furnishings. He takes the chair with a dominant athleticism that speaks of a desire to run wild, his legs spread wide, elbows braced on each arm as he leans forward.

I instinctively fold myself into my own chair, knees braced, ankles together, hands clasped in my lap. We could not be more different––he is totally at ease in his own body, uncaring of where he is; he's simply himself. I have spent a lifetime learning who I must be––sometimes I wonder if I have any idea what or who 'I' really am. Who might I have been had I not been born a princess? Who might I have become had circumstance not made me the sole surviving member of the royal family at seventeen?

He's looking at me, those eyes of his overtaking me for a moment, so I forget he's here at my request, that this is my meeting to shape.

'I've had a chance to review your proposal,' I say, careful not to give away my true feelings in the tone of my voice. It won't be helpful if he knows how much I don't want his casino monstrosity here.

'So I gather,' he drawls. 'And what did you think, Princess?'

'Please, you don't have to call me that.'

'And what should I call you instead?'

I'm not one to stand on ceremony, yet with this man I hesitate to invite him to use my name as I ordinarily would. I need every boundary I can establish between us. 'Most of my guests refer to me as Your Highness,' I clip.

'Is that any different to "Princess"?' His cynical expression reaches inside my tummy and squeezes it, so I look away, flustered and warm-cheeked. The river is placid, calmly meandering past the window. I watch it for a moment.

'It's more...what I am used to,' I say, forcing myself to turn back and face him, then wishing I hadn't when I find his eyes lingering on the necklace at my throat. Or are they actually lower, on the brief hint of cleavage exposed by the neckline of my dress? My pulse goes into overdrive. There's no denying how he makes me feel. It's like being flooded with electricity. I close my eyes for a moment, needing to regain control. When I open them, he's looking right at me.

My pulse speeds up.

A knock at the door is a welcome intrusion. I jerk to my feet, uneasy and tense, striding towards it.

Another staff member is there, holding a tray. She curtseys when she sees me, but before she can come in I hold out my hands to take the tray from her. I ignore her surprise, removing the sterling silver object and turning round in one movement. The door clicks shut, leaving me alone with Santiago.

I place the tray on a side table and remove the tall glass of beer, carrying it towards him with knees that are slightly unsteady. His eyes are sardonic as he extends a hand to take it. 'Thank you, Your Highness.'

Nope. That's no better. There's still something illicit and inflammatory about his tone. He might sound as if he's being respectful, but he's not, he's teasing me.

I double back to the tray, pouring tea from the pot then lifting the saucer and cup, holding them in my hands. I don't approach my chair. It's too close to the man, and there's nowhere to look but at him. Besides, sitting doesn't match my frame of mind. Instead, I walk towards the window, looking out at the river and the city beyond.

'The project is…ambitious.' It is not, by any stretch, the only word I can think of to describe his proposal. I hate everything about what he's planning.

'No more so than many others I've undertaken.'

'Yes.' I sip my tea. 'Your track record with this sort of thing is impressive.'

'Thank you, Your Highness.'

Another response that's lightly mocking. My spine is ramrod-straight and I cast him a look that I think barely contains my own feelings.

'It would be the first casino in Marlsdoven.'

'And you don't approve.'

Alarm bells sound in the back of my mind. Does he know about my uncle? Or is he simply hazarding a guess? 'Why do you say that?' There is a noise as he places his glass down. A cursory glance shows he's half-finished it.

'The negotiations are complete, your government ready to sign off.'

'It's crown land. The government can't sign off without my agreement.' It's a small, unthinking admission and I realise what I've said as soon as I finish.

'And for this reason you have organised a covert meeting at the eleventh hour to forestall the big, bad developer from corrupting your quaint kingdom?'

Fire spills through me. My lips part on an indignant rush of breath; I'm grateful to be holding the tea cup or I'm not sure what I might do with my hands! I cannot think that I have ever been spoken to like this, with such obvious disrespect, and such cynicism and dislike.

And how can he downplay the seriousness of this? I've seen first-hand what addiction can do! I know the evils that come from places like his casinos. If there is to be one in Marlsdoven, then the benefits had better far outweigh the risks.

'This is not a covert meeting,' I respond to the first charge, too emotionally invested in the second to trust myself to speak to it sensibly. '*Nothing* about my life is covert. Your name is in my daily schedule.'

His disbelief is obvious. 'I note I was directed to come to the back gate of the palace, brought through rear doors with no photographers in attendance.'

Heat prickles beneath my skin because his observation is accurate. While it's not exactly 'covert', I did try to keep the meeting off the press's radar. Spurred onto the defensive, I respond, 'Would you have liked to be photographed, Santiago?'

I use his first name and realise I like the taste of it in my mouth. I'd started to think of him as Santiago since seeing so many photos of him during my research. I don't care. We're beyond the bounds of etiquette now, anyway.

'My comment was more about your feelings than mine,' he says, neatly turning the argument on me, studying me as though I'm a science experiment. I remember belatedly the advice in the security report: he has a savant's genius when it comes to finding what makes people tick. 'I have no issue with being ushered into the palace like a shameful secret, but I find it telling that this was your choice.'

I open my mouth to object to this characterisation but change my mind. After all, why should I be ashamed of my feelings? 'I don't see the point in advertising your intentions to my people until we're confident the development is going to proceed.'

He reaches for his beer, takes a drink then replaces the glass on the table, standing in a lithe, graceful movement, walking towards me before I can properly realise what he's doing. I have no time to brace for his proximity. He's wearing an aftershave that sends my pulses into overdrive, but not enough of it, so I have to breathe deeply to catch the intoxicating masculine aroma.

Every hormone in my body is doing a dance.

'Your Prime Minister is desperate for this to happen.'

'Naturally. You're looking at spending billions of dollars. Of *course* he's keen.'

'This doesn't sway you, though?' he asks, looking around the palace as if to emphasise the wealth at my fingertips. If only he knew! Our small country is far from prosperous. The privatisation of most of our state-owned assets shortly after my parents' death, when I'd been too young, inexperienced and grief-plagued to understand what was happening behind my back, means much of our revenue is being paid to offshore companies.

'Selling crown land is a difficult business,' I murmur, remembering the lessons I learned as a seventeen-year-old. 'Once sold, it's gone. Everything needs to be structured so the advantages to the country outweigh the loss of such an asset.'

His eyes narrow. 'You don't think the casino will do that?'

No. Casinos are dangerous. I bite back the thought, knowing how counter-productive it would be to rely on this man's compassion and comprehension. 'I think it could,' I say with a small lift of my shoulders, my heart pounding as we draw closer to the crux of my argument. Somehow, he's brought me here without my realising it. I wanted to take time to charm him, to impress him with the country's history and cultural importance, to form some kind of rapport. But he's cut through all that and found the kernel of my reservations so easily, so skilfully.

'Then let's talk, Princess. What do you need from me?'

CHAPTER TWO

WHAT DO I need from him?

My mouth goes dry as I struggle to come up with any kind of answer. My brain is clogged, completely overwhelmed by him, my body overtaking all my instincts. So, instead of focussing on the simple business of the matter at hand, I find myself aching to reach out and touch him, to feel for myself if that broadly muscled chest is as firm as I imagine it is.

What the heck is happening to me?

I have made it through my entire adult life without going gaga for a man, and yet here I stand, with exactly the man I need to keep my wits with, and I risk turning into a blathering fool.

'Shall we go over your proposal?' I suggest, the idea literally going off like a light bulb, because if we pore over contracts surely that will negate the impact he has on me?

'Isn't that what we're doing?'

'I mean properly. At a table, with the documents. It would be easier to address my concerns this way.'

'We can do that,' he agrees, and it's then that I realise how totally he's taken the upper hand in this conversation. 'But first, I'd like to hear your concerns from you. Now. In summary.'

'Are you ordering me?' I can't help but respond, lifting a brow.

'Oh, never, Your Highness,' he responds with a hint of droll amusement. 'You're the one who gives orders around here.'

My cheeks grow warm again. 'You aren't like anyone I've ever met.' The confession escapes before I can stop it.

'I can imagine.' Again, I feel scorn layered beneath the banal response, as though my comment on his uniqueness has led him to derision for my place in the palace, the country.

'Meaning?'

'That your usual visitors are probably a very carefully curated type of person.'

My gasp is audible. 'Mr del Almodovár—'

'Santiago,' he interrupts, and if I liked the taste of his name in my mouth I love the feel of it in my ears even more. He says it with such Spanish tones, all sunshine and spice. My stomach clenches in overwhelming awareness.

'I think we've got off on the wrong foot,' I

say, searching for a modicum of control. 'You don't know me, and I don't know you. You're not here to get to know me, and I have no interest in knowing you. What I care about is my country, and the impact your casino mega-complex will have on the culture of the region.'

I look at him through narrowed eyes, my breath uneven. My dad flashes into my mind and I feel a stomach-clutching panic. I'm letting him down so badly. I wish there was some other way! 'So, perhaps we should avoid any personal observations whatsoever and move onto the contracts, as I suggested.'

'Are you sure avoiding personal observations is what you want?' he asks smoothly, and my whole body fires onto high alert. Heat builds low in my abdomen, spreading through me. My breasts are tingly and heavy, my nipples straining against the lace fabric of my bra. I turn away from him, afraid of how exposed I must be to someone with his experience. He's unpicking me piece by piece, stripping me raw, and I have no defence against him. More concerning, I don't know if I *want* a defence against him.

'You don't act like a man who's eager for this deal to go ahead,' I say, looking out at the river, seeking a sense of calm that won't come.

'No.'

'Why not? I thought this was important to you.'

'Oh, it is. But you are not the only one who does your research, Princess. I could walk away tomorrow and find another country to work with, many of which would be tripping over themselves to offer incentives to take my business there. But you? Could you find such an appealing investor as easily?'

I close my eyes on a wave of surrender, because he's right. Damn him. I feel actual hatred for the man then, and it's only intensified by the glorious, sensual awareness cresting through me. How dare he be the only man I've ever looked at and felt a stirring of desire for? No, not just a stirring, a total tsunami, a crushing weight of need that robs me of the ability to breathe.

'Not to put too fine a point on this, but you need me. So let's stop dancing around the issue and come to agreement. I want this concluded today.'

He's so dismissive, so infuriatingly arrogant, I whirl around to face him, all semblance of regal control dissipating completely. 'And you always get what you want, I imagine.'

His smile makes a flame flicker in my gut. 'Does that bother you?'

'You bother me,' I respond honestly.

His eyes widen with a brief glimmer of surprise, as though he wasn't expecting my answer.

'But I don't know why.' More honesty. I

frown. 'We should focus on the business at hand, and then you can consider this concluded.'

The air between us sparks with lightning bolts.

'I bother you because I am the opposite of you in every way,' he says, his meaning not clear.

But that's not it. I meet people who are different from me all the time. I celebrate difference and value diversity. This is not about difference, it's about desire, and how completely threatening is my reaction to him. It's as though my body, usually a trusted ally, has defied me in every way.

'Your proposed development is bold and—'

'Ambitious, yes. You've said.'

'Mr del Almodovár—'

'Santiago.'

I grind my teeth. 'Please, let me finish my sentence.'

He eyes spark with mine and then he dips his head in terse agreement.

'We have no casinos in Marlsdoven. This would be a first.'

'One of the reasons I selected your country for this project. You're primed for this.'

'You mean my citizens are "primed" to become good little gambling lemmings?'

His eyes narrow. 'Have you ever been to a casino, Princess?'

Heat rushes my face. Before I can answer, he continues.

'Of course you haven't.'

I don't want to analyse his tone or meaning.

'Do you think if I'd been to a casino I'd be more likely to look favourably on your project? I believe the opposite is true. Seeing one of these places would likely make me refuse to sell the land to you regardless of any benefits I perceive for the country.' I suck in a shaky breath. 'But I suspect that would be cutting off my nose to spite my face, and I've no interest in doing that.'

He lifts his hand, rubbing the back of his neck, the gesture separating enough of his shirt from the waistband of his trousers to reveal an inch or so of tanned, taut abdomen. My mouth goes dry, my heart in overdrive. I stare at his chest, my stomach in knots, my brain fizzing. I've lost my train of thought completely.

'How do you know if by your own admission you have no experience?'

The challenge drags me into the conversation again, but not fully. His arm drops, and so does the shirt. The sight of his flesh is buried in my mind, yet it's not enough. I have a yearning to see him completely shirtless, to see all his chest, the entire expanse of muscled abdomen. I blink hard, trying to clear the thoughts, the vision, trying to focus. My country needs my concentration right now. I can't be distracted just because he happens to be seriously attractive.

'The land you've chosen is valuable, historic and prominent.' I return the discussion to ground I'm more comfortable with, clearing my throat, vanquishing thoughts of his chest from my mind—for now.

His accent grows thicker as he defends his plans with obvious determination. 'This land is the obvious place for this. It's perfect for such a development.'

My eyes sweep shut on a wave of sadness. My own dreams for the piece of central real estate are impossible to visualise now. The arts precinct I wanted to commission—a testament to the cultural richness of Marlsdoven history and a space where children could go and be inspired to create—was now just a once-upon-a-time fantasy.

'And your prime minister agreed to the sale.'

'I know.'

'Yet you don't agree?'

'It's irrelevant,' I say quietly. 'Isn't it? Would you consider a different location at this stage?'

'Would it make you happy if I did?'

I stare at him, not expecting the question and with no clue how to answer.

'Or wouldn't you still have the same ideological issues then that you do now? You don't want a casino at all. Right?'

'I don't think that matters.' The words are numb, resigned. 'I'm in the minority. My Prime Minister and Treasurer assure me the parliament wholeheartedly supports your investment. I have no justifiable power to overrule them.'

'It's crown land. As you said, your signature is required on the contract.'

Is he throwing me a lifeline? Reminding me that I do hold some power here? For all that I feel he's reading me like an open book, I can't understand him at all.

'I'm not in the habit of going against my parliament.'

'You're a terrible negotiator.'

My eyes widen at the criticism and then, to my surprise, he smiles, his teeth baring, his expression changing completely. His eyes crinkle at the corners and it's as if the sun is blasting into the room. I grip my tea cup more tightly, but nothing can stop my knees from wobbling.

I stare at him, so entranced by his smile that it takes a moment for his words to settle in my consciousness.

'You *can* refuse to sell to me, Princess, and that's your leverage here. So let's pretend you didn't just say that and go back to your agenda. What do you want from me?'

My heart turns over in my chest. I finish my tea, placing the saucer on a side table before fixing him with a direct stare.

'I want…' I find it impossible to finish the sentence. Focus. Focus, for the love of God. He's staring at me, waiting, and the more he looks the more my pulse fires and my brain fuzzes. 'Assurances,' I haltingly add. 'That you'll employ ninety per cent Marlsdovens, in both the construction of the development and then in the staffing once completed.' Relief that I've been able to pluck one of my talking points out of thin air spreads through me.

'I've already made assurances that fifty per cent of the contractors will be locally sourced.'

'Fifty isn't ninety,' I point out.

His eyes lock to mine as if to say, *Oh, really?* but then his lips twist with the hint of another smile and my thoughts get scattered again.

'It isn't possible to guarantee that requirement.'

'Why not?'

'I can't say that your contractors will be the best, and I'm only interested in hiring the best.'

'You think we can't offer quality workmanship?'

'The "best" encompasses many things— quality, affordability, experience. I work with a group of architects based in New York.'

'Yes, and that can be your ten per cent,' I say, glad that I spent so long analysing the details of his proposal.

'What else?'

'Is that an agreement?'

'No. But I'm interested in your list. Go on.'

He's so close to me—just a foot or two away—yet I don't move. I should. I know I should. But standing here so close to him is hypnotic and addictive. 'My biggest concerns centre on the benefits of this agreement to my people. Once I sell this land, it's gone. I need to know the choice will benefit Marlsdovens for a long time to come. Particularly if the trade-off is having a casino right over there.'

I point down the river to the banks in question, my pulse quivering as I think of my father and how devastating this would be to him. My entire life revolves around doing what my parents would have expected of me, remembering every instruction they gave me over the course of my life. I'm betraying them now, and I'm sickened by that.

'It is more than a casino. The development features restaurants and a six-star hotel as well.'

'Yes, for guests of the casino.'

'Why do you oppose this?'

'I told you, I just need to make sure—'

'No.' He shakes his head. 'It's more than that.

You dislike the concept. You disapprove of the casino. Why?'

'It's just not something in our culture.'

'Gambling? I think you're wrong.'

'Gambling is everywhere, to some extent, but casinos make it so easy.'

'And that's bad?'

I stare at him. 'How can you not see that?' I shake my head, remembering what gambling did to my uncle, how his addiction led to his death. 'Of course you don't see it.'

'What's that supposed to mean?'

I realise I've gone awfully close to throwing an insult at his feet—worse, to blaming him for Uncle Richard's problem. I try to back-pedal. 'You made your fortune building casinos. Why would you stop and think about the ramifications on a society? Why would you see anything but good in these places that tempt and seduce people to fritter away their hard-earned money? How many lives have been ruined in your quest for this gambling empire?'

To his credit, he doesn't let my barb derail his argument. 'If I don't build this casino, someone else will—perhaps not on crown land, and then your approval will not be needed.'

'I'm aware of that.' It's the only reason I dismissed the possibility of refusing to sell to him. I'm fighting a losing battle, so I might as well

try to control it and get some benefits for the
people of this country.

'I want to know that the income from your
venture will fund health care and education for
my people. I want to know there will be employ-
ment prospects for future generations. I want
there to be world-class hospitality training available. Marlsdoven is haemorrhaging young citizens. They go to school here, but many then
move abroad for tertiary studies and stay there.
I understand the lure of your casino, Mr del Almodovár, and I understand that there are benefits. But I'm not going to stand here and pretend
I'm not highly sceptical of the whole operation.'

He looks at me for several moments and I
wonder if I've gone too far. I intended to im-
prove the deal with him, not ruin it altogether.
Is there a risk I've done just that?

'Your parents died seven years ago.'

It's the absolute last thing I'd expected him to
say. It's like an arrow coming out of left field,
spearing me with pain in my side. I blink away
from him, frowning as I take in the glistening
river.

'Yes.'

'You were seventeen.'

'Yes.'

'That's very young to assume such responsibilities.'

It's true. At seventeen, I felt grown up but, looking back, I was still a child. A child who'd had to grieve the loss of her parents and somehow hold together a grief-stricken nation as well. The need to be what my people required meant I never had the time or space for my own feelings.

'I managed.'

For a moment, before he dips his head in acknowledgement, I think I see sympathy in his eyes. I hate it. I don't want his sympathy—or perhaps it's more that I can't live with it. When anyone is kind to me I grow close to tears, and if this man, who came barrelling into the palace with such obvious animosity and disrespect, starts being *nice*...?

I cough to hide the fact I'm clearing my throat, not wanting him to register that I'm emotionally off-kilter.

'I can see you take your duty to the people of Marlsdoven seriously.'

I stare at him, waiting for him to make his point.

'This casino will benefit them.'

I hate that he's talking as though this is a *fait accompli,* even though I understand that it is. It must be. I can't go against the wishes of my country's Prime Minister and Treasurer. Frustration is like a whirlpool in my gut, swallowing me whole.

'Casinos benefit nobody,' I say caustically. 'Except, of course, the corporation behind the casino, which naturally stands to make gross profits from people's hope-filled gambling.'

It's the wrong thing to say. Anger flashes like a blade in his eyes, whatever sympathy I'd seen a moment ago evaporating completely. 'Yes, I profit from my casinos.'

'Not just 'profit'.' Now that I've started, I can't stop. 'You make tens and tens of billions every year. Honestly, what does someone even need with all that money? Don't you have enough? Is another casino in your empire really necessary?'

His eyes narrow.

'How do you sleep at night, Santiago, when the people who flood the floors of your casinos are living out their worst nightmare?'

'You have no idea what you're talking about.'

'Oh, yes, I do. I know damned well what places like your casinos do to families and lives.' I'm trembling with the force of my anger, Uncle Richard's haunted expression something I'll never forget. 'I hate everything about what you do. And I loathe the idea of selling this land to you.'

'What can I say, Your Highness? We do not

all have the advantages of being born into this.' He gestures to the palace, and contempt is encompassed in the flat line of his mouth.

I'm so tempted to tell him that being born into royalty is many things, but 'advantaged' is not one of them.

'No, that's true,' I say instead. 'Most people aren't royal.' I aim for sarcasm. It's small-minded and rude, but I don't think I care.

A scathing twist of his lips shows, if anything, my remark has amused him. 'You want to keep "your people" in the dark ages.'

'By saving them from the lure of gambling?'

He laughs, a thick, gruff sound that sends sparks of lightning through my body. 'Do you have any idea how prim you sound?'

I gape, the disparagement unexpectedly hurtful. I spin away from him, because I need the breathing space. He's too close, too everything.

'In every pleasure, there is the potential for pain. Should alcohol be banned altogether because some people have a propensity to alcoholism? Should driving be outlawed because there are some drivers who will always speed just for the thrill of it? Of course not. You cannot protect your citizens from every possible perceived evil. Life doesn't come with any guarantee.'

'That's just the sort of reply I'd expect from

someone who's never borne any personal responsibility.'

His head whips back, as though I've punched him. 'With respect,' he says it in a way that makes it clear the words are empty, 'You know nothing about me or my responsibilities.'

'I know enough.'

'Because I own casinos.'

'Because you own casinos,' I agree, my anger stirred beyond usefulness. 'Because you live the life of a hedonistic bachelor intent on drinking, smoking, having debauched parties on superyachts, all the while robbing poor people of their homes and relationships. I ask you again, how do you sleep at night?'

'Rarely alone,' he throws back, the words sparking through me, and I gasp, the image of him naked fully formed in my mind. 'But apparently you know that already, Princess.'

'This is getting out of hand.' My voice shakes, fury still ripe in my gut, disbelief at the direction our conversation has taken making my skin clammy. Or is it the reference to his sexual activities? I press fingertips to my throbbing temples, willing myself to calm down.

'You are the one who's letting a personal opinion interfere with a business proposition.'

'That's not true.'

'Then how come the way I live my life doesn't bother your Prime Minister or Treasurer?'

My eyes sweep shut at his very valid point. 'Of course it bothers them. They're men of integrity and you're…you're…'

I whirl around to face him, only to find that the Spanish billionaire has closed the distance between us. He's right behind me, his eyes latched onto mine, his face a mask of repressed emotion——but I see beyond it. I feel the fury emanating off him in waves.

'*Si?* What am I?'

'Not like them,' I finish lamely, my anger cresting and falling, being replaced by something else now, a different wave, something more dangerous and distracting. I stare up at him, my body quivering with a thousand and one things.

He's so close, though, so close, and I find myself slipping, my fingertips tingling with a need to *feel.* I clasp them together in front of me to stop myself doing something really stupid, like reaching up and running them over his chest.

I know I should move away. Take a step backward. Put some space between us. But being near him is doing something vital and addictive to my body; it's resonating through me.

I hold my ground, inches from him.

'No.' His expression is grim, his eyes piercing mine before dropping to my lips, tracing the line of my mouth until I open it on a small gasp. A gasp or a plea? I can't be certain. 'I imagine they never argue with you like this.'

I shake my head wordlessly, just the tiniest movement, for fear of dislodging his gaze from my mouth. I feel as though he's touching me. Pleasure spikes through me. I have no idea what this means—I've never seen a man and longed for him in this way. It's wrong and inappropriate, but even that knowledge makes me want him more, not less. 'No one does.'

Something like understanding flashes through his eyes. 'And do you like being argued with?'

'Of course not,' I lie, ignoring the fact that I feel more alive right now than I have in my entire life.

His soft laugh shows he understands, and it embeds itself in my nervous system. 'Then shall I leave?'

Yes. Yes, he should. This conversation is counter-productive, his presence an affront. We're never going to agree. He should absolutely leave. 'I…' The words are jammed in my throat, some invisible barrier preventing them from escaping.

Triumph crosses his expression. His eyes shift to mine, a challenge in their depths as he lifts a hand, moving it closer to my face. I hold my breath, staring at him, waiting. He touches his fingertip to my cheek, phantom-like, so I shift a little closer, pressing my cheek to his palm. What's happening to me? How can I possibly be doing this? I'm the Crown Princess of Marlsdoven and this man represents a serious threat to my country. Yet here I stand, entranced, captivated, pleasure exploding through me.

'Come to Spain with me.'

The invitation is husky, his voice deep and accented. I blink, not understanding. His finger inches lower, towards my lips. I have to swallow back a groan. 'I can't.'

'Come to see my casino there. You cannot truly form an opinion on the merits of my proposal until you have witnessed one for yourself.'

My eyes sweep shut, reality intruding on the fog of awareness that has momentarily incapacitated me. It's a timely reminder of who he is and why I have to fight this drugging attraction with everything I have. I snap out of my haze, pulling away from him, jerking backwards, trying to load anger into my eyes. 'I know enough.'

He's surprised by my rapid shift, but surprise quickly morphs into determination. 'Are you afraid to be proved wrong?'

'There's no chance of that. I'll never approve of gambling.'

'Casinos are so much more than gambling,' he insists.

'Next you'll be telling me people play with tokens and no real money is ever wagered.'

'There's no fun in that,' he drawls sardonically.

'There's no fun in people losing their money, gambling until their debts get out of control.'

'No,' he agrees. 'And we have safeguards in place to try to prevent this.' He closes the distance between us. 'Come to Spain and see for yourself.'

My heart twists, my ability to think clearly impeded once more.

'Or are you afraid of what will happen once you leave this gilded cage?'

I blink up at him. 'Afraid?'

'Just you and me, no rank, no staff—no reason to ignore what we both clearly want.'

CHAPTER THREE

HIS WORDS POUND through my mind with the force of a sledgehammer: the challenge, the assertion, the statement of intent. A *frisson* of danger and need runs down my spine. I stare at him for a long time, losing myself in the vortex he's created. I need to say something to set aside his ridiculous suggestion.

'My rank goes where I go, I'm afraid.'

'Then I'll call you "Princess" at all times.'

It's a sensual promise that does little to calm my raging bloodstream.

'Santiago...' His name is a plea, but for what?

'Your Prime Minister and Treasurer do not oppose this development because they know what you do not: this development is good for your country, your people, your future. And while, yes, there are some down sides associated with casinos, mine is probably the only casino group in the world that actively provides gambling support and interventions. But I think you're afraid to be proved wrong.'

'I'm not afraid of that,' I deny swiftly.

'Then what are you afraid of?' Has he moved closer? Our bodies are almost touching. My breath is uneven, loud in the silent room. 'Or do I even need to ask?'

'I'm not…'

Now it's my turn to stare at his lips. Of their own volition, my eyes drop to his mouth, chasing the outline, and such raw, primal need surges through me that I make a soft, gasping sound. It's as though I can will him to kiss me.

Kiss me?

Alarm spears my side.

I can't seriously want…

But, oh, I do.

'You despise me,' he says gruffly, his body position changing just enough for me to feel as though he's forming a wall around me. I like it. 'You despise my life, my choices, my business.'

I don't deny it. Not because it's true—though it is—but because I'm not capable of following A to B right now. My thought train has been completely derailed.

'But right now you wish that I would kiss you on those perfect pink lips of yours.' His eyes spark to mine, daring me to contradict him, daring me to say that's not what I want.

'So?'

A short, sharp laugh of surprise breaks between us, and then his head lowers, his face only an inch from mine. 'Come to Spain with me.'

It's the last thing he says before he kisses me—the first kiss of my life and it's with this man who, as he just pointed out, I despise.

I've seen enough movies to know what it's like to be kissed—or at least I've imagined it. But this blows every expectation way out of the water.

My stomach is in knots, looping over and over. My body is paralysed and then on fire as he lifts one hand to the back of my head, his fingers driving through my hair, holding me where I am as his mouth ravages me—there is no other word for it. His lips separate mine, his tongue lashing me, demanding answers I can't give, showing me his supremacy. I whimper into his mouth, a sound of acquiescence and surrender, a sound that hopes for more of this—him—so much more. The kiss drives down into my soul. I am in agony but an agony born of the knowledge that this kiss is not enough. My hands lift to his chest, pressing to his warmth, the rock-hard muscles just as tantalising as I'd imagined.

I curl my fingernails into the fabric of his shirt and he kisses me hard, his knee nudging my legs apart so I groan, the unexpected contact so unmistakably sexual, so hot, so raw, that I can't think or speak. I am floating high above the planet, and nothing matters besides this.

Alarm bells clang in the back of my mind. I *know* this is wrong, so wrong, but I'm powerless to stop it, held hostage by a body that has been denied any form of sensual pleasure for far too long. As a teenager I read romance novels and, oh, how I loved them. Yet that zing was never for me in the real world. I've never met anyone with the ability to set my soul on fire.

But Santiago del Almodóvar, with his charismatic devil-may-care attitude, is the very last word in hot and, like the many, many women who've no doubt come before me, I have no desire to resist him.

He pulls away, just enough to break the kiss, his eyes probing mine. 'Spain. Come next week.'

'Next week,' I repeat, my mind not following.

'Stay at the casino. Experience the type of building I want to bring to Marlsdoven.'

I nod, but it's not an agreement. My brain is too fogged to think straight. Belatedly, logic starts to fall into place. 'I can't.'

'Then stay somewhere else.'

'I can't come to Spain.'

He frowns. 'Why not?'

'Because it would…arouse suspicion? I don't know.'

'Suspicion of what?'

My cheeks flame. His smile is mocking and I feel about three feet tall. I shake my head in frustration, desperately trying to re-establish a modicum of control, to put some cool between us. But his leg is between mine, his body still so close, our faces separated by only an inch. My breath burns in my lungs and my nipples tingle against the fabric of my bra. My insides feel like mush and warm heat is spreading through my abdomen. I am lost.

'It's just not like me to go somewhere on the spur of the moment.'

'This is not spur of the moment.'

'A week is… My schedule…'

'Do not make excuses.'

'I—I'm not.'

He presses a finger to my lips then steps back, separating from me with apparent ease. He is not flustered. He is not breathing as though he's just run a marathon. He looks at me with a steadiness I envy.

'This is business. You have concerns about the development? So come and see what I do. Come and experience my casino and hotel. Eat at my world-class restaurants. See for yourself what I am proposing to build here.'

I bite down on my lip, because his suggestion actually makes a lot of sense. But it would involve being in Spain with Santiago and that kiss definitely complicates things.

'I—have to think about it,' I say, not quite meeting his eyes.

'Then think.' He shrugs his shoulders with nonchalant ease. 'And let me know.' He paces towards one of the occasional tables, withdraws his wallet and leaves a card on the surface before striding towards the door. I stare at him, frowning. Is that it?

I don't want him to leave. I want…

But what I want is impossible. Or at least highly inadvisable. I need him to go so that I can start to think straight.

I hold my breath, waiting for him to turn and say something to me, to reassure me, placate me or even to walk back and kiss me all over again, but Santiago is done. He draws the door inwards and leaves the room without a backward glance.

My heart is thumping so hard I genuinely worry it could crack my ribs into tiny shards of bone.

'And? How did it go?'

I look at Claudia with a furrowed brow. Where to begin?

Claudia is my senior advisor. I've known her

since I was a teenager. She's ten years older than me almost to the day, which as a teenager made her seem quite grown-up, but as I've reached my mid-twenties I think of her almost as my contemporary.

Though our life experiences are quite dramatically different. Whereas I am sheltered and, I freely admit, naïve, Claudia is worldly and sophisticated. She takes two months' holiday every year and goes back-packing all over the world, far off the beaten track. She is fearless and courageous, determined to see every pocket of the earth. A month ago she got back from Nepal and her stories of hikes and cuisine have been feathering my soul ever since.

'It was fine.' I reach for a glass of water, taking a long sip, my throat burning at the lie.

'Oh? I'm surprised.'

'Why?'

'Because he's renowned for being difficult. I would have thought you'd butt heads a bit, particularly given your reservations.'

I look at her for several seconds and then sigh. 'We *did* butt heads.' Unconsciously, I lift my fingertips to my lips and, despite the fact he left the palace hours ago, they tingle at my touch. My body feels half-electric. I don't know when or how I'll ever feel *normal* again.

'And yet you resolved it?'

'Not exactly.'

Claudia frowns. 'I thought the contracts were to be signed today?'

'No.' I toy with my fingers. Am I letting my people down by stalling? The boost to our economy from this project would be tremendous, not to mention the flow-on effects for the tourism industry. The whole riverbank precinct would be revitalised by this development.

It's just not the kind of revitalisation I want.

I understand the economic benefits of his development, but whenever I think of my parents I shudder. This would be an enormous betrayal of their memories, and the promise I made myself right after they died. My mother used to tell me there was no blueprint for being a crown princess, but she's wrong. I have a blueprint—my parents' actions—and I want to adhere to it. But turning away Santiago when his development shows such promise for our economy? Guilt and indecision gnaw at my gut.

'So when?'

I lift my shoulders, then turn to Claudia.

'What are you not telling me?'

Too much. Yet, although I have a habit of being completely honest with Claudia, I clam up now. What happened between Santiago and me is something I need to make sense of in my own time and in my own way. I can't discuss it.

'I might have spoken too frankly with him,' I say quietly. 'I was quite forceful in my objections.'

'To the project?'

Heat marks my cheeks.

'Oh, Your Highness…' She shakes her head, her green eyes sparkling. 'Don't tell me you called the incredibly wealthy Spanish tycoon some unkind names?'

I grimace.

'I can imagine his ego wouldn't have liked that. Particularly when he's used to women tripping over themselves to fall at his feet.'

I grab onto that, my breath uneven. 'Do you think he's really such a…?' I search for the right word.

'Oh, yes. A total man-whore,' she supplies with an impish grin. 'I think he's every bit as bad as the press says, and then some. Trust me, I've known men like him before.' She wiggles her brows. 'And, while they're fun to spend time with, you definitely can't trust them as far as you might wish to throw them.'

I am not a jealous person but, illogically, I feel the blade of that emotion cutting through me.

'I don't think he's ever had a relationship that's lasted longer than one night. Probably more than one hour.' She winks, no idea how those words are tightening something in my chest. It's so stupid of me to feel like this. All those romance novels have predisposed me to ideas that make no sense. Besides, in less than a year's time my own engagement will be announced—to the man my parents dearly wanted me to marry. Never mind that I've met him only a handful of times and feel nothing for him whatsoever. That doesn't change the fact I have no business fantasising about Santiago, or being jealous of his sleazy flings.

Except…the way he kissed me is *all* I can think of. I don't care that he goes through women faster than most men do underwear. I liked the way it felt to be kissed, the way it felt to be touched, the way it felt to be spoken to as an equal.

My eyes flare wide as I realise that's a huge part of this. Santiago didn't revere me, he didn't 'ma'am' me. He ignored all the conventions and spoke to me like any other person, and I loved that.

'He wants me to go to Spain to see his casino in Barcelona.' I ponder, the idea having more weight with me than I'd allowed him to see.

'It's not a terrible idea,' Claudia responds.

'Really? I'd have thought you'd object.'

'Oh, to anyone else I'd say that if you've seen one casino you've seen them all. But you've never been inside a casino before—'

'With good reason,' I mutter.

'I know you hate the very idea.' She's sympathetic. 'But I don't think this is a fight you really want to pick; it's definitely not a fight you'll win. So why not go and see his hotel and try to talk yourself into feeling good about it all?'

Except it's not the casino that's playing on my mind so much as the way it felt to be kissed by Santiago. In a matter of months, my engagement will be announced, my marriage will take place only a few months after that and then the rest of my life will be lived according to the blueprint my parents set out. I've never questioned that fate but, for the first time in my life, I have an insatiable hunger to experience something outside of what's expected of me.

My days are always scheduled. Everything in my life is planned. Right down to who I'll spend my time with. What if this is the last chance I'll ever get to do something spontaneous and 'normal'?

The idea is seductive, almost as seductive as the thought of seeing Santiago again away from all this—the palace that reminds me at every turn of my parents and their legacy.

'I don't think it would create the right image,' I point out, almost hoping she'll contradict me and save me from myself.

'So don't let anyone know.'

I roll my eyes. 'Yeah, right. I'll just slip through the airport security unnoticed. Me, my luggage and four security agents.'

She laughs. 'The agents don't have to sit with you. As for being recognised…' She stalks to my wardrobe and returns a moment later, carrying a baseball cap. 'Try the time-honoured tradition of dressing in disguise.'

In order to keep the visit low-key, Claudia arranges everything. She alone deals with my diary secretary, booking the flights and accommodation, ensuring my schedule simply states 'personal trip'.

I wait until everything's locked in before I draw Santiago's card from where I stashed it on my bedside table, dialling his numbers with fingers that aren't quite steady. As the phone begins to dial, my stomach swoops, so I pace to the window and stare out at the banks of the river, reminding myself this is business. At least, that he doesn't know this will be a last-ditch and first ever taste of freedom for me. That the idea of escaping from my life for a few days holds an immeasurable appeal. It's nothing to do with him, really, so much as him being the first man to flirt with me so brazenly, the first man to kiss me with such obvious hunger.

As soon as he answers, his voice rolls through

my body like sensual heat and honey. My knees tremble.

'Del Almodovár.' His voice is gruff, accent-spiced.

'Santiago.' I clear my throat. 'It's Freja Henriksen. From Marlsdoven.' I cringe at my own awkwardness.

A beat passes and then there's the sound of a door closing. 'Your Highness.' His surprise is evident. 'How are you?'

My heart turns over at the question—a normal, polite, civil enquiry.

'Fine.'

'I'm glad to hear it.'

A woman's voice interrupts in the background of the call. I cannot make out what she's saying—t's too fast, her Spanish fluent, whereas mine is only passable—but I hear enough. It's a woman, it's late at night and I can only guess what I've interrupted. My heart goes into overdrive, my stomach in knots.

Claudia's appraisal of his bedroom antics plays in my mind. I'd be a fool to forget—even for a moment—what he's all about.

'Perhaps I should call back at a more appropriate time?'

I wince at my icy tone and can just imagine his smirk in response.

'Why is this not an appropriate time?'

Of *course* he'd call me out on this instead of just letting it slide. I expel a sigh. 'It doesn't matter. This won't take long.'

'Go on.'

My heart thumps. 'I've decided to take you up on your offer.'

'I see.'

'Is that a problem?'

'To clarify, which offer?'

I frown. 'To come and see your casino in Barcelona?'

A beat passes.

'You do remember suggesting that?' I prompt.

'Oh, yes, Princess. But there was another offer we discussed that afternoon, if memory serves.'

Heat spirals through me, and indignation too. Of all the cheek! He really *is* as bad as Claudia said. To proposition me while he's with another woman! 'I don't remember that,' I respond with saccharine sweetness. 'But, rest assured, seeing your casino is *all* I'm interested in.'

His laugh is soft. 'We'll see.'

Warning bells chime.

'I'll have the presidential suite made available.'

'That's not necessary. My aide's arranged everything. Oh, And Mr del Almodovár?' I intentionally use his surname, wanting to undo any expectation he might have that this trip is about more than the casino. 'My visit is to be of a secret nature. I don't intend to tip anyone off that I'm coming and I'd appreciate it if you'd do the same.'

'You're so ashamed to be seen in one of my casinos?'

'In any casino,' I correct, wondering why I'm being so rude to him. After all, any other business contact would warrant a modicum of respect, yet with Santiago I'm deliberately baiting him.

And enjoying it.

And do you like being argued with?

'Fine. I'll ensure your privacy is respected. A car will meet you at the airport.'

'That won't be necessary.'

'When do you arrive?'

For a moment I contemplate not telling him, but that would be somewhat churlish. 'I'll have my assistant email some details. But don't worry about freeing your schedule. I won't need much of your time. After all, I'm coming to see the casino and not you.'

Another laugh, deep, short and throaty. 'I get the picture, Your Highness.'

My insides roll with unmistakable desire. I know he's doing it to mock me but the way he keeps using my title is making my pulse go nuts.

'It's just—not something I want to advertise to my—'

'Your people, I know.'

Something tightens inside me. He could never understand what it's like to live like this. The expectations and speculation, the constant fishbowl nature of my life.

'I'll see you later, then,' I say, but don't hang up.

And, interestingly, neither does he.

'Santiago?'

Oh, great. Now what am I going to say?

'*Sí?*'

Who are you with? The words tingle on the tip of my tongue but I force myself to swallow them away. His social life has nothing to do with me. The kiss we shared was a mistake, an aberration, something I won't allow to happen again. I *can't* let it happen again. There are so many reasons for this man to be off limits to me. Not least because I genuinely, chemistry aside, can't stand him!

'It doesn't matter. I'll see you soon.'

CHAPTER FOUR

IN THE END, I'm able to wangle a trip with only two security agents, and they keep a distance from me, so that as the plane lands in Barcelona and I walk down the steps, sunglasses and baseball cap in place, I feel anonymous and free. So free.

It's a warm afternoon and a light breeze lifts off the runway. I smile spontaneously, looking around before being swallowed by the milling passengers all bee-lining for the terminal. I join the crowd, happy to be absorbed by them, thrilled to have been unrecognised so far. The terminal building is air-conditioned. I flash my passport—with a brief moment of discomfort as the customs worker clearly identifies me and bows, but fortunately no one else seems to register his strange response.

Once through customs, I follow the signs to the baggage hall, taking in every detail of this pedestrian travel experience. Compared to the usual fanfare of my trips, this is low key and low stress. The noises that swirl around me are new—conversation and play, children running, adults scolding. There is none of the muted, carefully managed interaction I generally experience.

I want to remember every single detail!

In the baggage hall, I frown, not sure how to find my suitcase, but one of my agents approaches. He's also dressed casually, to blend in, and I can't help but grin at the sight of him in jeans and a T-shirt rather than the customary suit.

'This way, Your Highness.'

'Remember, Alex, I'm just Freja for the duration of this trip.'

He lifts a brow in silent scepticism then gestures with his hand. I walk alongside him but freeze. Standing at the carousel and sticking out like a sore thumb is Santiago del Almodóvar.

I stop walking so abruptly that one of the children who'd been playing around bumps into my legs. I ruffle the child's hair apologetically then keep walking, my pulse in my throat, my mind in overdrive.

Santiago was not dressed particularly formally the first time we met, but now far less so, in faded black jeans and a grey shirt with the sleeves rolled up to his elbows, the hem untucked. He wears a baseball cap and a pair of aviator sunglasses. With his forearms exposed, I notice that he has tattoos. A snake on one arm spirals around and around towards his wrist, where its head appears to be biting the base of his thumb. The other bears a sentence in cursive script. I can't make out any detail from this distance.

'Would you mind getting my bag, Lars?'

'Of course, madam.'

'Madam' is a compromise I can live with. I stalk towards Santiago, my stomach doing loop-the-loops.

'What are you doing here?'

He lifts off his aviator glasses. 'Isn't it obvious?'

My heart thumps.

'I came to get you.' He pulls off his hat. 'I even brought a disguise but I can see you've got that covered.'

I stare at the hat, then him, consternation zipping through me.

'You came to get me?'

Great. I'll just parrot everything he says. That won't make me seem like an idiot at all.

'We're a six-star hotel, remember? All service.'

'I'm not… But…'

He lifts a finger to my lips and I'm instantly

reminded of the way he kissed me at the palace. Possessively, with ease, as though he had every right. But he doesn't. I'm not one of his one-night stands.

I jerk my face away then step backward. 'Don't.'

His eyes glint like onyx in his handsome face.

'I have agents here.'

'And what? You're threatening to set them on me if I touch you?' he drawls and, despite everything, I laugh, shaking my head.

'That's not what I meant.'

'I know what you meant.' He leans closer and lowers his voice. 'You're fine to kiss me in a room where it's just the two of us, but not for anyone else to know you find someone like me attractive. Right?'

'I didn't have you pegged as the insecure type,' I respond, his accuracy felling me.

'Not insecure. Amused. I cannot imagine living my life with so much concern for what others thought of me.'

'Obviously,' I respond tautly.

'Your bag?'

'My agent has it.'

'And does he also have the address of the hotel?'

I nod. 'Of course.'

'Good. Then he can follow behind.'

He puts an arm on my elbow, guiding me from the crowd. I stop walking, perfectly aware that if it looks like I'm being abducted my cover will be blown in about seventeen seconds. I turn around and sure enough see my guards running towards me, one with his hand reaching for his gun.

I shake my head quickly. When they're close enough to hear, I say, 'This is Mr del Almodóvar, my…host. I'm going to travel with him.'

'But Your Highness…'

Our earlier compromise about using my title is forgotten.

'It's fine,' I assure Alex. 'I trust him.'

They don't like it, but this whole trip is unorthodox enough that they grudgingly nod.

'We'll drive behind you. Where are you parked?'

He gives them directions then begins to propel me from the airport once more, and this time I let him. His fingers press into the small of my back, his touch insistent and strong.

We're crowded by others in the lift and he stands close to me, his body behind mine, his warmth enveloping me, his fragrance unmistakable. I breathe in, grateful for the anonymity of being able to close my eyes and cope with his nearness, for those few vital seconds to pull myself together before the doors ping open and his deep voice says, *'Perdóname'*, causing people to separate and make way for us.

I'm used to a degree of subservience wherever I go. People 'obey' me—I hate that term but I can't think of any other way to describe it. But the responsiveness here is all down to Santiago. Whether he's recognised as one of the country's wealthiest men, or simply exudes that air of authority wherever he goes, I see the way his words are taken as a command. Even my security agents were quick to fall in with his suggestion.

His car, naturally, is sleek and black, a beautiful sports car with heavily tinted windows, a golden badge I don't recognise on the bonnet. The headlights flash as we approach. He surprises me with his manners as he comes to the passenger door and opens it for me. When I move to step inside, he puts a hand on my arm. Every part of me goes haywire.

'I'm glad you came.'

My stomach twists. I stare at him, right back to where I was a week ago, torn between what I want and what I know I must do, how I know I must act.

My smile is tight, my body hot. 'It's a good opportunity to appraise your casino. Thank you for suggesting it.'

The suggestion of a smile plays on his lips.

I feel his cynicism and slip into the car before I can say something else, drawing the seat belt into place.

He rounds his side, flaring the engine to life a moment after taking a seat. The car instantly feels smaller, his presence overpowering. I am conscious of the strain of his trousers across his thighs, his hyper-masculine fragrance, his capable hands on the wheel. He tilts me a sidelong glance, then checks his rear-view mirror. A car is approaching, black with windows tinted just as dark as these.

'Your staff?'

I flick a glance in the mirror as Alex puts down the driver window so I can identify his face. I nod. Santiago puts the car into reverse and backs out in one swift, easy motion, then accelerates forward. With every rev, I feel the car's power beneath me, thrilling and raw, just like Santiago. His hands shift the gear stick as he drives, so my eyes are drawn to his fingers, tanned and confident, and his leanly muscled forearms. At the bottom of the car park, he presses a button and the driver window lowers, allowing him to tap his phone to the boom gate. It opens in response, but he waits on the other side, conscious of the security agents, allowing them time to come through behind us before he accelerates into traffic.

I've been to Spain before, but there's something about being here like this—incognito, no official schedule of visits, no state engagements, undercover and unknown—that makes the whole outlook glisten with magic. The buildings are at first industrial, but as we draw nearer to the centre I see the hallmarks of this famed city. Baroque buildings in various states of repair are juxtaposed with modern constructions and Renaissance churches remain, their stone features beautiful, the perfect contrast to the Gaudi and Gaudi-influenced buildings we zip past in the city centre.

We drive through a restaurant precinct, the buildings close together, with red awnings and flower pots adding bursts of colour. The street is paved and narrow, so Santiago slows down, and I glimpse tables all set to face the street, the umbrellas dotted around to ward off the sun. Diners are dressed with casual elegance, and suddenly I long to be amongst them, eating tapas and drinking wine, making conversation with like-minded friends. A pang of longing assails me for the type of simple friendships most people take for granted.

'A sigh?'

I spin to face Santiago, a frown pulling at the corner of my mouth. 'Excuse me?'

He turns to look at me and my breath catches

in my throat. His eyes are as golden as the Barcelona sunshine today, framed by thick, dark lashes. Those freckles on the bridge of his nose draw my attention.

'You sighed.'

'Oh.' I swallow. 'It's just—this looks so lovely.'

His eyes shift beyond me to the tables strewn with afternoon diners.

'We can come here for dinner.'

My spine jolts with warmth. It's not a dinner invitation. It's so much more intimate than that. It's a presupposition that we'll share a meal.

'I came to assess the casino,' I remind him primly, already forgetting that this is also, in part, a chance for me to kick up my heels—discreetly, of course. 'Dinner on the streets of Barcelona, while charming under different circumstances, is unnecessary.'

His eyes hold mine for a moment longer and then, with a slight smile, he turns back and continues driving. The world beyond the car has lost its ability to hold my attention. All my focus is now on Santiago.

'Is there something in your royal rule book that precludes fun?'

Despite the question, I smile. 'Sorry to disappoint you, there's no such thing as royal rule book.'

'Isn't there?'

The question is insightful. I sigh again, a soft exhalation of breath this time. 'There are…conventions and expectations,' I murmur. I don't explain to him that my life is guided by the expectations of my parents; he'd probably mock the sentiment, and I don't think I could bear that.

'And these rules mean you cannot come for dinner with me at a restaurant like this?'

'I wasn't planning on having dinner with you at all, actually.'

His laugh is a throaty sound.

'Why is that funny?'

'Because you are determined to act as though you don't want to spend time with me when we both know that is not true.'

And his hand shifts off the gear stick and towards my knee, grazing my skirt lightly so I startle, my veins immediately rushing with lava.

'I was warned about your arrogance,' I mutter, hoping I sound dismissive.

Another gruff laugh, a bark of noise. 'I'm sure you were.'

He shifts gear and my gaze flickers lower.

'You have a tattoo.' I change the subject without really meaning to. He's unnerved me by being so breathtakingly honest—and beautiful!. 'Two of them.'

'I have more than two.' The look he shoots me is pure sensual invitation. My heart stammers.

'Santiago…' It's a breathless complaint. 'Listen to me. What happened between us the other day…'

'When we kissed?' he prompts, once again tilting his face to mine, a knowing look in his eyes.

'Right.' I brush it away but my lips tingle and my soul aches. 'It was a mistake.'

'Oh?' He hits the indicator then turns the car off the road, taking us towards the beach. The water shimmers like diamonds in the distance, the sun bouncing off it. He skilfully navigates a narrow one-way street then takes us across a busy road, turning one corner and then another, checking the rear-view mirror to be sure my detail is following.

'Definitely,' I murmur, toying with my fingers in my lap.

'You don't like to be kissed?'

I briefly imagine how he'd react if I told him that that was the first time I'd ever been kissed.

'It's not appropriate for *you* to kiss me.'

The only sign he's heard is that his knuckles briefly turn white as he grips the steering wheel more tightly, before sliding the car down a ramp towards an undercover car park. I notice a steel-and-glass monolith above us and my mind immediately fills in the gaps—it's his casino, the building he had designed and constructed some ten years ago when, at twenty-one, he was a self-made billionaire and already the envy of Europe.

'Why not?'

'Because.'

'That's not an answer.'

So what is an answer? That I don't have the freedom to simply kiss any man I find desirable? That I'm supposed to marry some man my parents picked out for me before they died? That I owe my country more than to become one of Santiago's lovers, a single woman in a long line of women to have graced his bed?

'Let's just chalk it up to experience and leave it at that.'

He swings the car into a parking bay right next to the lifts.

His eyes lock with mine and the air between us thickens, sparking with electricity. I feel as though I'm being sucked into a vortex of awareness, every inch of me reverberating with need.

Desire sparks like a fever in my blood, propelling me forward, but only by an inch; despite what I've just said, I want him to close the gap. My lips part, my breath is held, and my eyes are on his at first, then on his lips, tracing their outline as I remember what it felt like to be held in his hands and ravaged by him.

'You want me to kiss you right now.'

The words are a statement of fact. I contemplate denying it, but pride won't let me lie.

'What I want and what I know to be right are two different things.'

'And wanting me isn't right?'

I shake my head a little, and somehow end up closer to him, my body almost touching his now. My seat belt strains across my chest but the pleasure of that physical contact is like a placeholder for him. I imagine his hands on my thighs and at my shoulder, and shiver.

'Why not?'

In the distance, there is the banging of car doors. My security detail. Their approach makes me feel urgency.

'Because,' I hiss, my heart pounding. 'You're you, and I'm me.'

'What does that mean?'

'In a year's time I'm going to be the Queen of Marlsdoven. Even if I wanted to do what you're suggesting...' heat rushes my cheeks... 'I can't. I'm not at liberty to have meaningless affairs. My people expect more of me.'

'So how do you conduct relationships, then?'

He seems genuinely interested, the look in his eyes speculative rather than sensual.

I focus on my knees. I wonder what he'd say if I told him the truth. He'd probably be shocked, then bolt out of the car faster than you could say, 'I don't sleep with virgins'. The idea has my stomach squeezing—for all that I know a relationship between us is impossible, I don't want to turn him off completely.

'You don't know what it's like,' I say after a beat. 'I'm watched *everywhere* I go. In the palace there are staff, and outside there are citizens who see me, by virtue of my birth right, as "theirs". There's an ideal of what a princess should be and all my life I've been taught to live up to it.'

'And what happens if you don't?'

The question is one I've never asked myself. 'I don't want to find out.' My expression feels heavy with regrets. I press my hand on the door handle. 'Thank you again for coming to get me.'

His eyes pierce me for several long seconds, but before I can open the door he reaches out, pressing his fingers over my knee. 'Dinner tonight. In your hotel room.'

My lips part on a rush of breath. 'No.' It's too intimate.

He reaches for my chin then, holding my face steady, our eyes latched. There is a plea in my heart, a plea for him to understand how difficult this is for me.

'*Sí.* Don't fight when you don't want to, Princesa.'

Princesa. The word heats my blood, my eyes sparking with his. His hand drops from my face and regret forms like a brick in my gut.

'I suppose it would give us a chance to go over some details of your development,' I say with a small lift of my shoulder, not meeting his eyes in case he sees the fib for what it is.

To his credit, he doesn't gloat. 'Tonight, then.'

A shiver runs down my spine, but not one of fear. No, this is a response of anticipation and warmth, a tingle of excitement at what lies ahead.

CHAPTER FIVE

WE DIDN'T ARRANGE a precise time for dinner, a fact I'm only cognisant of when eight o'clock comes and goes and there's still no sign of Santiago. I've been waiting for him for almost an hour and I feel frustrated, annoyed and more than a little disappointed.

To my chagrin, my hotel room reservation was upgraded to the presidential suite despite my insistence that it wasn't necessary, and the suite is far, far bigger than I could possibly want. Several sumptuous bedrooms, each with their own bathroom, as well as a spacious living room that features a white grand piano, marble tiles and golden curtains framing floor-to-ceiling windows. There's a fireplace as well, for those wintry nights, though it's hard to imagine Spain being cool enough to warrant such a thing when the city is as it is now—bathed in the last rays of the summer sun, warm and golden, glowing with a hint of magic.

There is a kitchen too, and a cursory inspection when I first arrived showed it to be fully stocked with Spanish delicacies. I'm contemplating making myself a little platter of olives and bread when, finally, a heavy knock sounds at the door. I know without looking that it's him, but ingrained training has me waiting right where I am. A moment later, the door opens and Alex announces Santiago's arrival. Alex's expression is impassive yet I can't help but wonder and worry about what he might make of this turn of events.

That concern doesn't last long. The moment Santiago steps into the suite, my mouth goes dry and my mind empties of all considerations that don't revolve around him.

He's wearing a dark suit now, casual in its styling, with a crisp white shirt unbuttoned at the throat revealing a hint of dark, curling hair, just like the first day we met. He shrugs out of his jacket as he strides closer to me, discarding it over the back of a chair, revealing shirt sleeves pushed up to show his tanned forearms.

'Hi.'

I utter the greeting simply to fill the silence. My heart is thumping heavily.

His only response is to walk towards me, and I can't help but notice his taut waist as he moves, the shirt fitted to reveal his strength and raw power. I remember the way it felt to be in his arms, and the way his body had been hard and warm. Desire weakens my knees, and my determination.

I look away, but it doesn't help; he's imprinted on my mind. When he's close enough that his fragrance tickles my nostrils I turn back to face him cautiously. His eyes are heavy on my face, and a spark bursts between us as I meet his gaze.

'How was your afternoon?'

My afternoon? I have to rally myself to focus. 'I… Fine.'

'You walked through the gaming floor?'

I lift my brows. 'You're spying on me?'

'You are not the only one with security guards.'

I frown. 'You have security?'

He dips his head. 'Particularly when I'm at the casino.'

That makes sense. His net worth is stratospheric, which must put him at risk. I just can't imagine anyone targeting Santiago—more fool them.

'And *they* spied on me?'

His lips curl in a sardonic smile. 'Actually, I advised them you were here so that they could ensure your safety.' A hand lifts, his fingers lightly brushing my cheek, robbing me of breath.

Danger sirens blare.

'It's a precaution we take with any high-value guest.'

My heart twists. I tell myself to step backward, yet stay exactly where I am.

'The point of this trip was to fly beneath the radar.' My voice is husky. 'Hence I travelled on a commercial airline, booked an ordinary room…'

'But you are not ordinary, Princesa, no matter how you try to behave. And I do not want the publicity that would result if harm were to befall you in my casino.'

Disappointment sears me, as well as a sense of foolishness at my own expectations. Of course this wasn't about me. He was only looking after his business and its reputation. 'You don't need to worry about me.' I belatedly take a step back, needing space.

He lifts his shoulders. 'As I said, it's a precaution we take with any prominent visitor.'

'Nonetheless, it's not necessary.'

He shrugs, and I know there's nothing I can say that will change his mind. 'They're discreet. You didn't notice them today, did you?'

I hadn't, but that's not the point. I can sense the futility in arguing with him, though. Besides, he's right. If he wants to waste resources having his own security guards trail me around the venue, then that's his decision.

'Fine.' I move into the kitchen, tapping my fingers on the bench top. 'Would you like a drink?'

The question is curt, my temper at risk of fraying, as it seems to be almost all the time that I'm around Santiago. I can't explain why I feel so deflated suddenly.

His face look shows a hint of mocking amusement. 'I can't have you waiting on me, Princesa. What would your people say?'

I turn to the fridge. 'Contrary to what you might think, I'm perfectly capable of pouring a glass of wine.'

'I wasn't sure if you drink,' he murmured, coming jarringly close, swinging the fridge door open and removing a dark-green bottle.

'Only when I'm not working.'

His eyes probe mine and I realise—too late—what I've just admitted. That tonight isn't about work.

My fingers twist at my sides but he doesn't make a big deal of it, simply side-steps me to remove a couple of tall-stemmed glasses from the cupboard. He pours a little into each, a very reserved amount, before handing one of the glasses over.

'What is it?'

'A Godello.'

I lift the glass to my nose first, breathing in the aromas before taking a sip, closing my eyes to fully appreciate the floral explosion, perfectly balanced with tartness and acidity.

'It's gorgeous.'

His laugh is hoarse. 'I am glad you like it. I have just enough grapes to make a small vintage each year. This is the two thousand and twelve.'

'You make the wine?'

'It's a hobby of mine.'

I blink at him in surprise.

'You didn't expect this?'

'Frankly, no.' I take another sip. Somehow the fact this man has been involved in its creation adds even more depth to the wine, so it hums as it moves through me.

'Why not?'

'I suppose I see you as someone with more frivolous hobbies.'

One of us, or perhaps both of us, has moved closer; there's barely any gap now. The air is thick.

'You think I'm frivolous?'

'No. I think you're...' I search for a word, shaking my head in frustration when one won't come to me. 'Your lifestyle is well documented.'

'A few photographs of me on a yacht and you

think you know everything about me?' The question is light in tone, his manner seeming easy and amused, but I understand the depth beneath his question, and there's a hint of something in his eyes that makes my skin prick with goose bumps.

'Is that image wrong?'

His smile is laced with tension. 'No, *querida*.' Now it's definitely Santiago who moves closer, his powerful body dwarfing me, framing me, making me feel whole and laced with adrenalin. 'I like women.' He takes a sip of his wine then places the glass on the counter top. 'I like sex.'

I gasp at the truth of that statement, and the way it sets off a chain reaction of desire all through my body. Fascination spears through me.

'I also like making wine.'

The final sentence comes to me as if from a very, very long way away. I nod, but I can barely focus.

'And what are your hobbies?' he prompts in a gravelled tone that makes me wonder if he cares what my answer is. After all, are words necessary now? Everything between us is sparking and my body is throbbing like the beating of a drum, its urgent tone pushing me forward.

'I don't have any hobbies,' I say simply.

One dark brow quirks in surprise. Somehow he moves closer, and now we're almost touching.

'I don't believe that.'

'I'm not lying to you.'

'Everyone has hobbies. Interests outside their work.'

'My work is my life,' I say softly. 'Or perhaps I should say, my life is to work?'

He *tsk*s under his breath. 'That sounds very dull.'

'Of course it's not,' I lie. 'I take my responsibilities very seriously.'

'As evidenced by your squeaky-clean reputation,' he says with a nod.

'Have you been googling me?'

'Of course.'

My heart thumps. It's been a long time since I've searched myself on the Internet but I can imagine what's written there. Nothing. No speculation about my love life, no speculation about anything, because I never, ever stray outside the lines of the palace that have been drawn for me, lines my parents stressed the importance of observing.

'You are an excellent princess, much loved by everyone.'

'Yet you sound unimpressed.'

'Because you're living a lie.'

I gasp at the statement, so certain, so hurtful.

'Am I?'

'Your life is one of calm and measure, your smile cold, your dress so formal.'

My lips part, poised to ask a question, but I never get a chance to form it.

'Yet you are not cold, you are not calm. At least, you are neither of these things when I kiss you.'

And, before I can guess his intentions, he does just that—dropping his head, his mouth claiming me, his lips pushing mine apart as our tongues clash, our bodies welded together. He kisses me until I'm everything he just said—the complete opposite of calm and cold.

My body is flushed with awareness, my nipples almost painful against the confines of my bra and my insides squirming with need, heat pooling between my legs. My feet refuse to stay on the ground; one lifts and locks behinds his legs, clamping him to me as my hands lift and intertwine behind his neck, pulling him to me. I'm half-terrified he might stop kissing me now he's made his point, and that's the very last thing I want.

His hands shift to my hips, holding me there, drawing me to him. I moan low in my throat, the power of his erection impossible to ignore, striking power and a hint of fear into me, because I've never done this before, and it's all I can think of. Kissing him is sensual and perfect but it's not enough. I want so much more.

Driven by an ancient rush of feminine power, by instincts that are an essential part of my soul, I pull up against him at the same time he lifts me, perching me on the edge of the bench. I have a vague recollection of his wine glass being somewhere nearby but I'm incapable of connecting the dots and breaking apart from him to move it. To hell with it. Other things are far more important right now. My fingers curl into the hair at his nape, pressing my breasts to his chest, and his hands at my hips find the fabric of my shirt, lifting it to reveal a bare stomach, then going higher to my bra. We separate, purely so he can rip the shirt off my head and toss it to the floor at his feet; it's a momentary, necessary pause and then his mouth is back on mine, dominating me, awakening me…

'This is who you are.' He pushes the words into my mouth at the same time he unclasps my bra, so my breasts spill out, only to be caught in the palms of his hand. There's pleasure in his possession, a thousand arrows darting through me at the intimacy of this contact. I have never been touched like this but it doesn't feel strange. On the contrary, it feels perfect and right, those same instincts removing any hint of uncertainty. *This is who you are.*

I can't analyse his statement, I can't read into the truth or otherwise of it, because I am only capable of feeling right now. But, yes, every feeling in my body convinces me of what he's said. This is who I am. I have never felt more authentic, more real, than right now, laid bare and vulnerable to this man, yet powerful too, because the fabric of an ancient ritual is over-taking my soul.

His fingers glance across my nipples and I groan, pleasure spreading through me, a desire unlike anything I've ever imagined, much less felt, eliciting a drugging sense, like the beating of a drum over and over and over again.

He drags his mouth from mine, lavishing kisses on my collar bone then shoulders, before taking a nipple in his mouth and flicking it with his tongue until my breath becomes laboured, my breathy cries filling the room. I feel him smile against me, then his stubbly jaw shifts sideways, his mouth tormenting my other nipple as his hands cup my bottom. He lifts me effortlessly from the kitchen counter and carries me through the suite, his stride long and confident. His mouth finds mine again and his kiss obliterates thought.

This is his hotel, his presidential suite; he finds his way to the master bedroom easily, shouldering open the door and crossing the plush carpet to the bed in the centre. He lays me down gently, his body coming with mine, barely breaking the kiss. It's only when he shifts to remove our clothes completely that we pull apart, but there's not enough time for reality to fully intrude. I'm glad. Reality might bring with it caution and sense, reasons to avoid this, but the truth is, I can't.

I've never known this heady rush of longing before. I've never felt desire, chemistry, sexual need. I've never felt a spark of attraction, let alone this. One day soon I'll be Queen and I'll be formally engaged to a man I barely know and certainly don't desire. My future has been laid out for me from birth with no room for deviation. A reality I have long accepted suffocates me now, and the only relief is in this tiny act of defiance, a small, inconsequential indulgence of my own needs before I assume the duties of a kingdom.

Santiago is a man who takes women to bed without much forethought. This means nothing to him, and it will mean nothing to me either. It's just sex. But it's sex with someone *I* choose. It's all my choice. Not the requirement of my country, the will of my parliament or the sensible need for a royal heir.

A spirit of revolution hardens my resolve, so

I know now that wild horses couldn't draw me away from this.

As if sensing the direction of my thoughts, he hovers above me, standing. His chest has a tattoo of a bird flying just above his heart, and there's more cursive script running across his hip. His chest moves with the ragged drawing of his breath, his eyes probing mine. 'You're sure?'

'Yes.' It's a husky, hungry acceptance of what will and must be.

His eyes glitter as he spins away from me. Rustling his trousers from the floor, he flicks open his wallet and removes a condom. 'I never take chances,' he explains.

I amuse myself with what he'd say if I told him I'm a virgin, that sex with me is completely safe—before the penny drops and I realise he's alluding to children, an unintended, lifelong consequence of a reckless night of passion.

'No baby del Almodovárs on the horizon for you?' I murmur as he rips open the foil square and rolls the condom over his arousal. My eyes cling to the action, and I'm jarred out of my slumberous, all-encompassing desire because of his obvious size.

His smile tilts the earth off its axis. 'Definitely not. I never intend to have children.'

I'm curious as to his reason. I have never given this issue any thought, for the simple reason that having children is yet another purpose of my existence. As a royal—the sole surviving royal of my house—I have been aware for a long time that I must have babies, and several of them. I don't know if it's what I would have chosen otherwise, but a cursory examination shows that I like the idea. I'm more excited about being a mother than I am about being a wife.

There is no more time to analyse this. He brings his body over mine, his smile gone, his expression hauntingly beautiful as his knee nudges my legs apart, his body weight on mine a pleasure in and of itself. His kiss is slow at first, his tongue languorously exploring my mouth, my breasts tingling beneath his hair-roughened chest, my fingers tracing his tattoos by memory, a question in every strike of my touch. I am lost, buried under the weight of need, full of wanting him. I'm unable to think, breathe, talk so that, when he nudges the tip of his arousal against my sex, I can only groan in the base of my throat. There is no time for anticipation or fear; he drives into me, his full, powerful length hard, strong and dynamic, pushing past the invisible barrier of my innocence, his body possessing mine for the first time.

He freezes, bracing himself on his elbows. His eyes meet mine, surprise obvious on his face, a question in his gaze.

'Freja…' My name is squeezed from between his teeth. Is that an accusation I hear? Anger? Briefly, darkness eclipses my pleasure, but then he begins to move again and any hint of discomfort his first thrust invoked dissipates, leaving only pleasure in its path. Intense, soul-destroying pleasure.

He is skilled and intuitive, driving me to the brink of ecstasy many times before drawing me back, tormenting me with his easy mastery of my body, showing that he can control my pleasure with ease.

I don't know how long he does this for, but it's long enough for me to feel delirious with desire, a heat building inside me that is crazy for release. I plead with him over and over, his name on my lips a garbled cry until he kisses me, weaves our fingers together and finally tips me over. He drives me over the edge of awareness, heaving me from this earthly plane so that I'm in freefall, conscious only of surrender—his and mine—as his body is racked with breaths, his strength throbbing inside me. A guttural cry rents the air before he kisses me once more, murmuring Spanish words I don't understand into my mouth.

Tears burn my eyes and I can't stop them. The sheer perfection of what I just experienced defies explanation. I know people talk about sex, and I got that it's meant to be amazing, but I had no idea it could be so completely earth-shattering.

I blink to clear the tears, not wanting him to see them, needing a moment to gather myself even as he's still buried within me.

He pushes up onto his elbows to look down at me, scanning my face and, I'm sure, seeing far more than I wish to expose.

'And so the Princesa was a virgin,' he murmurs, a hint of something in his face I can't comprehend.

'Was it that obvious?'

'To me.'

My heart stammers. It occurs to me that I must have been pathetically boring after the women he's used to sleeping with. He kisses the corner of my mouth, taking my self-conscious fears with him. 'Did I hurt you?'

I shake my head. 'At first, a little. But no. That was…' I search for the right word, then smile.

'Freja.'

I blink, because it's unusual for him to use my name rather than my title. I like hearing it on his lips, in his accent. 'If I had known, I would never have pursued you.'

'Why not?'

His own features tighten. 'Because a one-night stand is a very different consideration than being someone's first lover. I have very little interest in the latter, generally.'

'Then I'm glad you made an exception for me.'

He doesn't respond to my quip.

'The reason I like one-night stands is that there are no expectations beyond great sex.'

His logic baffles me. 'Whereas the fact I'm a virgin means I must now be expecting a proposal?' I tease, smiling to show how wrong he is.

His eyes are wary. 'Or at least a relationship of sorts,' he clarifies carefully.

'I can't have relationships,' I say simply, the words hiding a pain buried deep in my heart, a pain born of jealousy for what I see as 'normal' for most of the world.

'That makes less sense to me now than when you first said it.'

'Think about it, Santiago. My life is an open book. Where would I meet someone? How would I date them? Break up with them? Heaven forbid I dated several men. My country is conservative, and the royal family is seen to be perfect, beyond reproach. I could never expose myself to that kind of gossip. I would never disgrace my parents' memory.'

'But surely behind closed doors…?'

'There are very few closed doors in my life,' I say wistfully. 'I live in a palace that has hundreds of servants. They are good people, but still people, and people gossip. If a boyfriend snuck into my apartment at night, word would quickly get out, and before long articles would appear in the press.'

'And would that be so bad?'

'It's easy for you,' I say with a sigh. 'You don't care about stuff like this. Look at the stories that are written about you! The press loves to report on your lifestyle, your over-indulgences, on the fact you're a "bad boy".' I smirk, because it's such a perfect description of this man. 'You could never understand how much I would hate that.'

'I don't love it,' he replies, surprising me with his honesty. 'But nor do I give it much thought.'

'But my job is to be the Queen my people deserve. That's incompatible with the lifestyle you're suggesting.'

'I'm not suggesting you roll from one wild party to the next, but only that you might have dated from time to time.'

'It's not possible.' If it's strange to have this conversation while our bodies are still joined together, it doesn't occur to me. 'And particularly not now.'

'Why not?'

'Because next year my coronation will take place, and directly afterwards my engagement to His Royal Highness Heydar van Anjers will be announced. It would be highly inappropriate for me to date anyone right now. So please don't think that this…' I run my fingers down his side '…is going to complicate your life in the slightest—virgin or not.'

CHAPTER SIX

'YOU'RE ENGAGED?'

It's not the reaction I'd expected, and nor is the darkening of his face; there is a look there I can't interpret.

'"Betrothed" is a more accurate description,' I explain as he pulls away, shifting to lie on the bed beside me, a frown etched on his lips.

'What is the difference?'

'Well...' I consider that a moment. 'To say we're "engaged" makes it sound like we've been dating and decided to get married. Whereas I've only met Heydar a couple of times. Our relationship isn't—and never has been—romantic.'

'Obviously.' He pushes up onto one elbow so he can see me better. His scrutiny is unnerving. 'So why the hell are you marrying him?'

'Because we're betrothed.'

'Meaning?'

'Meaning that, a long time ago, his parents and my parents, who were very dear friends, entered into a contract binding Heydar and me. The terms were crystal-clear. On my twenty-fifth birthday, our engagement would be announced, with the wedding to take place no more than three months later.'

He says something under his breath, something Spanish, and I guess from his tone that it's a swear word. I blink up at him, unsure of his reaction.

'What is it?'

His dark eyes probe mine for several seconds.

'Frankly, I don't like the idea of having slept with another man's fiancée.'

I laugh, because it's so completely unexpected. 'I just told you, we're not engaged. It's not like that. Besides, I'm sure he's not letting our arrangement stop him from seeing other women.'

'And it's okay for him to date, but not you?'

I sigh dramatically. 'That almost sounds like there *might* be a double standard for men and women,' I observe with a fine peppering of sarcasm. 'Men are expected to have girlfriends. It's old-fashioned and it sucks, but he doesn't have the same expectations to be morally beyond reproach that I do.'

'How can you accept such restrictions so calmly? I'd want to burn the house down.'

'It's my life,' I say with a shrug.

'But it doesn't have to be.'

'A second ago you looked half-terrified I was going to latch onto you and beg you to spend the rest of your life with me, and now you're trying to talk me out of going through with my wedding?'

'I can feel both those things,' he assures me. 'This is an academic discussion; it has no bearing on what just happened between us.'

I wonder at the slight pain in my chest, as if a blade's pressing against my heart.

'So why did you sleep with me?'

The question barrels towards me like a freight train. The answer is right there, glaringly obvious, but I feel that to admit the truth to Santiago would lay me bare. I angle my head a little, pretending fascination with a painting across the room. The art work in this suite is a blend of classic and contemporary—there are pieces from the Renaissance juxtaposed with paintings featuring bold, bright colours, abstract and happy-making.

His fingers touch my shoulder lightly, sending goose bumps across my skin.

'Freja?'

My name, again. My heart slows.

'Why did *you* sleep with *me*?' I push the question back on him, angling my head to his so I can see his expression.

His eyes scan my face with indolent ease, studying me, before his lips flicker in a quick grin. 'You're sexy.' He moves his finger lower. 'And beautiful.' He draws his finger towards my belly button, then makes a circle, running his finger around it again and again. 'And I wanted you.'

I wanted you.

The words bounce around inside me, the certainty behind them filling me with surprise. 'And that's how it works, is it?'

He waits for me to continue.

'You see someone you want and what—they fall into your bed?'

'Most of the time,' he drawls jokingly, but something a lot like jealousy flashes in my gut. It's not jealousy of *him*, it's jealousy of his freedom and lifestyle. 'You didn't answer my question, Princesa.'

I nod slowly. 'I wanted you too.'

'But you must have wanted men before. Why me, now?'

I prop up onto my elbow, mirroring his body language, my fingers lifting to the bird tattooed above his heart. It's an eagle, bold and confident, watching me as though with a warning in its eyes. 'You're sexy and beautiful?' I tease.

His lips flicker in another slow smile. My heart twists.

With uncertainty slowing my words, I say, 'Actually, I haven't.' I clear my throat. 'Met anyone I wanted before, I mean.'

At the look of triumph in the depths of his eyes, I roll mine. 'Don't let your head get too big, Santiago. I didn't exactly have much of an opportunity to meet anyone.'

'You've met men before,' he points out. 'Lots of men, I'm sure. And yet I am the only one you've ever been tempted to sleep with.'

It's one hundred per cent true, but I suspect his ego doesn't need the stroking.

'Whatever.' I flick his tattoo.

He laughs, a hoarse sound that sends little arrows of desire across my spine. Silence falls between us, warm and pricked with awareness.

'I guess,' I say thoughtfully, surprised at how honest I'm prepared to be with Santiago. 'I didn't want to miss this opportunity.'

He waits for me to continue and I order my words with care.

'I don't know much about Heydar. He seems nice, and he has a good record on all the things that matter. But, the handful of times we've been in the same room, I've felt nothing. Not even curiosity. We don't have any spark whatsoever. I'll marry him because he'll be good for my country, and because it was important to my parents, but I already know that our marriage won't have chemistry.'

I shift my hand to the snake inked on his toned forearm, tracing its length.

'And then I met you, and you were so infuriating and rude and direct, and unlike anyone I've ever known,' I say with a weak smile. 'And when you kissed me I felt like part of me I didn't know existed was being brought to life: and not piece by piece, but all at once, in a huge, fiery rush. It terrified me,' I murmur. 'I didn't come to Spain expecting we'd sleep together. In fact, I came determined that we wouldn't. After all, I can't be involved with someone like you,' I point out matter-of-factly. 'The way you make me feel is both exhilarating and terrifying. But I'm going to marry a guy I feel nothing for, so don't I deserve this?'

It's a rhetorical question. I'm telling him to absolve me of a sin that I haven't really committed. I'm telling him to understand.

He mulls it over for a moment before leaning forward, brushing our lips together. 'Everyone deserves great sex in their life, Freja. I'm just sorry you're willing to walk into a lifetime without it.'

It had never really bothered me before. If anything, I'd come to the conclusion I was asexual, not remotely interested in men. But now? Having been awoken by Santiago, what will it be like to push this part of myself back into the box?

Necessary, I remind myself. My country needs this, and it was the wish of my parents.

'How long are you in Spain for?'

'Four nights. Including tonight.'

'It's not long.'

'It's long enough to appraise the casino,' I point out, reminding us both of the main reason I came to Barcelona.

His smirk pulls me apart from the inside out. 'Sure.' His accent rolls over the word, softening it. 'But perhaps not enough to make up for lost time.'

I frown. 'What does that mean?'

'That we have four nights to give you a lifetime's worth of sexual satisfaction. It's a challenge, but I think I'm up for it.'

'That's big of you.'

'If you say so.' He winks at my unintended *double entendre*.

'You seriously have an ego the size of a house.'

'Is that all?'

We're quiet. Our eyes clash. 'The thing is…' I move my hand back to his eagle tattoo, then press my palm to his chest. 'I meant what I said before. I can't date. And I especially can't date you.'

'Because if people discovered we were sleeping together, a scandal would follow?' he says speculatively.

'Well, yes.' I bite down on my lip, worried about offending him before I remember this is Santiago del Almodovár. 'With everything that's printed about you in the press, my people would be horrified.'

'I have no interest in ruining your pristine reputation, Your Highness.' For a moment, I'm reminded of his antipathy on that first afternoon we met, the silent undercurrent of disapproval that was obvious in his every remark. But then he stands, extending a hand to me, so I place my own in his and he pulls me to standing. Our bodies are so close, my hips brush his.

'Four nights in my bed, and no one will ever know.'

Something like adrenalin courses through my veins. A secret affair with Santiago del Almodovár explodes through me; wonderment fills my body. It's not what I expected when I came to Spain, but it's absolutely perfect. Why shouldn't I enjoy a fling with a bad-boy sex god before I go back to Marlsdoven and continue to act like the perfect Princess the country expects me to be?

'Isn't it technically my bed?' I ask with fluttering lashes.

'Your bed, my bed. Let's not argue over semantics.' He scoops down and lifts me easily, cradling me to his chest. 'So long as there's a bed and you're in it, I don't particularly care about anything else.'

He runs the loofah over my body, sponging me until I'm covered in soap, the warm water of the shower rinsing it off. I watch him unashamedly, fascinated by this intimacy, by his closeness, by the fact he's not intimidated by me and by the way he reveres my body, worshipping me as though there is some all-powerful energy source layered beneath my skin. When I'm clean all over, he looks up, his dark eyes hooded, his expression causing my lungs to burst with air pressure.

'How do you feel?'

Better than I've ever felt before. 'Good.' I smile shyly.

'And here?' He presses a finger to my sex so I jump, the touch unexpected and perfect.

'Good.' I thought I was shy before!

'You're sure?'

I nod but, when he presses his lips to my most intimate core, I almost jump out of my skin.

'Santiago…' It's a plea, but for what?

He flashes his eyes at me, a smile playing about his lips before he moves his tongue, flicking my sensitive cluster of nerves until stars dance behind my eyes. I lift my hands up and press them flat against the tiled wall behind me, desperate for the support. The warm water douses my naked body, cascading down my breasts as he lashes me with his tongue… Then I'm falling apart at the seams all over again, pleasure a tidal wave drowning me in desire and, though we are taught to fear drowning, I can't say I feel anything right now but ecstasy.

'Did you grow up here?' I reach for another of the Cambados oysters, their ocean-salt flavour delicious, particularly when paired with Santiago's wine.

He watches me eat then runs his hands over his jaw, as if lost in thought…or weighing something up, perhaps. 'I grew up in the Ciutat Vella.'

'The what?'

'The Old City.'

'Ah. It sounds beautiful.'

His smile is sardonic. 'Does it?'

'Wasn't it?'

'There are parts,' he concedes.

'But not where you grew up?'

'No.'

'Why not?'

He reaches for an oyster, lifting it expertly to his lips and sliding it into his mouth, swallowing it whole. I'm transfixed, watching as his Adam's apple shifts in his stubbly throat.

'We lived in a crowded apartment building— one bedroom for the three of us. It was loud and untidy.'

My frown is reflexive. It twitches on my lips before I can stop it.

'Your parents didn't have a lot of money?' I prompt quietly.

'That is one way to say it.' He reaches for his wine and takes a sip, his eyes holding mine over the rim of the glass so bubbles of warmth spread in my veins.

'I hadn't realised. I knew that your fortune was self-made, but I presumed your parents gave you a start.'

'No.'

I nod slowly. His reluctance to expand is something I should probably respect, but curiosity fires through my belly. 'So what did?'

He waits for me to clarify.

'How did you get to have all this?' I gesture to the view of the city beneath us, the lights twinkling in the evening light. On the balcony of the presidential suite in his central casino, I feel as though the world is at his—and my—feet.

'Hard work.'

I laugh. 'That tells me nothing.'

'Doesn't it?'

Our eyes meet and I nod slowly. I can tell that he's a hard worker. Despite his party-boy reputation, I see beneath it—there is a streak of ruthless determination that convinces me Santiago will stop at nothing to achieve his ends. Even now, with hundreds of billions in the bank, he will do whatever it takes to ensure his next venture is a success.

Including sleeping with you? I push the horrible, insidious thought away before I can give it any credit. How ridiculous. Sex isn't why I'll agree to his casino proposal. It has nothing to do with it.

'I was on the brink of dropping out of school.' He surprises me by continuing, his voice raspy, as though the past is grabbing hold of him. 'I barely went anyway, not more than a few hours a week.' He casts his eyes towards the black void in the distance, at the ocean beyond the city.

'Why not? What did you do instead?'

His eyes pierce me with their intensity. 'I worked, *querida*.'

'You were just a child.'

'A teenager, and we needed the money.'

He reaches for another oyster. I shift to a horizontal position on the comfortable outdoor sofa, lying on my side so I can see him, propping my head on my palm.

'Besides, I hated school.'

'Really?'

'Doesn't everyone?'

'Oh, I loved it. Not school, but learning. In another life, I should have been an academic. Give me a pile of textbooks and a long test at the end of it, and I'm set.'

His laugh is throaty.

'No skipping classes for you?'

'No such luck. I had a tutor.'

'Of course you did.' His voice is droll, and again I'm reminded of our first meeting. His cynicism is most apparent when we touch on the trappings of my position. I push up a little and reach for my wine, taking a small sip. The breeze is warm, rustling over my hair, and I relish the sensations—cold wine, satisfied body, warm flesh. 'And of course you did not need to work to support your family,' he adds, so I feel almost a hint of guilt in my chest.

I shake my head before lying back down again. 'You didn't drop out, though?'

'No.' He studies me. 'A teacher saw me working at mechanics.'

Great. Now I have to imagine Santiago as a grease monkey, his head beneath the bonnet of a car, dressed in a white singlet and form-fitting jeans. My mouth goes dry.

'He realised I'd been ditching school to work

and hauled me into his office. I was surprised he cared, at the time. The school was not known for its academic reputation, and no one had given much of a care about what I did until then.'

Something about the throwaway comment makes my heart ache for him.

'What about your parents?'

His smile is tight, cautiously dismissive. 'That's another story.'

'I'd like to hear it.'

He shakes his head once; it's obvious he doesn't intend to elaborate. 'The teacher's specialty was maths. He set me extra work. Pushed me. I had an aptitude.' His expression bears the ghosts of the past. I perceive the pain that dogs him and wonder why I didn't comprehend it at our first meeting. Because he'd come in all guns blazing, and all my instincts had been askew, thanks to the way he'd made me feel.

'About three months after he started working with me, there was a phantom-stock-market game. Do you know what this is?'

'Like playing the stock market with fake money?'

'*Si.*'

'And you were great at it?'

'I earned over a million euro in the first week,' he says. 'So, yes, you could say that.'

My eyes widen. 'Seriously?'

His head shifts in a single nod. 'I was fifteen and had never had enough money in my life. We were dirt-poor, Princesa, and suddenly I'd been given the keys to a world beyond my comprehension.'

'But that was just pretend. How did you take that and turn it into all this?'

'I found investors, charged a scaling percentage of what I earned for them. It was their money, their risk—all the up side was mine.'

I shake my head from side to side, admiration filling me.

'I was able to diversify, invest in properties then major ventures, such as this.'

'You make it sound so easy.'

'Once I was given the keys, it was.'

Pleasure has seeped through me. I am exhausted and satiated. It occurs to me that I'm happier in this moment than I've ever been.

'And now, Your Highness, I must go.'

It jerks me out of my reverie. 'What? Why?'

His smile is arrogant and hot. I don't care that I've shown how much I enjoy his company, or that my disappointment is blatantly obvious. 'I have a meeting.'

I reach for my phone, checking the time. 'It's almost midnight.'

'And, in a casino, that's prime time.'

My face probably shows what I think of that. 'It's the middle of the night.'

His laugh is laced with mocking humour. 'So prim,' he teases as he stands and walks towards me, his body brushing mine when he sits on the edge of the sofa, our hips connecting.

Pride be damned. 'Do you have to go?'

'Yes,' he says, but I don't think I'm imagining the regret in his voice now. 'Besides, it is better if I don't stay the night. Your guards might do some of that gossiping you are so afraid of.'

He's right but I don't know if I care right now. I lower my eyes, painfully aware of what a hypocrite that makes me.

'Sleep naked,' he says gruffly. 'And dream of me.'

CHAPTER SEVEN

MY PARENTS WERE close to my uncle Richard. They adored him. My father's younger brother, he'd had all the advantages of royal life and none of the pressure and expectations that had weighed down my father and which had ensured he was sensible in his life choices.

My uncle had been free to do as he wished, largely left alone by the media. My father told me, when I was only small that at one time he'd envied his brother that freedom. He'd wished he'd been born second, able to live without the scrutiny and watchfulness of the world. And, while I can understand that sentiment, it was not borne out by history.

Uncle Richard had grown up without expectations and therefore he'd never striven to meet them. And, worse, he had everything he could ever want in life, so even the basic pleasure of aspiring to achievement had been denied him.

What could he do that would make a difference to anyone?

His gambling addiction had grabbed hold of him before anyone had known—the amount of money he'd lost eye-watering. I wake with my uncle in my mind and the sting of tears in my eyes, a sense of betrayal tightening around my chest.

How can I be making this deal? How can I be sleeping with the man who wants to bring a casino to my country?

It takes me a second to realise that I didn't wake up by chance. There is knocking at the door. I push the covers back, my heart racing in the hope it's Santiago. I wrap a silken robe around my body—yes, I slept naked—and pull the door inward.

A hotel staff member stands there, one of my guards at his side.

'Room service,' he offers in accented Spanish.

'Oh.' I take a step back, gesturing towards the marble-topped dining table. 'Thank you.'

It takes him a moment to wheel the trolley into position, placing it beside the table, then unstacking plate after plate of food, each covered in a golden lid. My attention drifts to the sunlit vista beyond the window, the sheer size of Barcelona fascinating me and giving me a desire to explore. In the distance, the sea glistens with shades of turquoise and aqua, so beautiful, particularly on a clear, sunny day like this. Impatience bursts through me. Impatience to be alone and free.

It's the first time in my life I've felt like this.

I nod as the waiter leaves, waiting until the door is closed to begin lifting lids off the platters. Fruit, Danish pastries, and an omelette filled with smoked salmon and drizzled with hollandaise sauce, as well as hash browns and sausages. It's too much food. There are two plates left to uncover. I pull the lid off one, frowning as I reach for what's beneath. Definitely not food. My fingers run over something soft and brown. Closer inspection reveals a chic wig. Beneath it is a brightly coloured scrap of fabric—a bikini.

Heat flushes my cheeks as I open the final lid to find a note from Santiago.

Meet me at the marina at midday. Wear the disguise. Bring the swimmers.

I stare at the bikini with a thudding heart. It's turquoise in colour and, so far as bikinis go, not too revealing. But the idea of wearing something like this...

I quickly shove it back onto the plate and replace the lid. I'm ravenous after last night—we ate only oysters and expended a lot of energy— and eat my way through the fruit and omelette, sipping orange juice and coffee, before tackling a Danish for good measure.

When I travel on official trips, my schedule is usually packed from morning to night. What a strange and pleasurable change this makes. I have nothing on the horizon, the day is my own. Or perhaps it's Santiago's...

Once more my eyes find the sea and something like excitement lifts my heart. For three days, I've escaped my normal life—no press, no intrusions, no pressure. I can do what I want, so long as no one finds out...

The car brings me to the biggest boat in the marina—naturally—a white yacht the size of several houses with tinted windows and several decks. I stare up at it from the back seat of the limousine, conscious of the wig hanging tight around my ears and the Lycra of the bikini against my skin. Naturally I'm wearing more than just the bikini—in fact, to the outside world, I look demure and business-like in a pair of cream trousers and a simple lime-green shirt tucked in at the waist. My shoes are flat, but definitely not boat shoes: in my defence, I didn't anticipate yachting as part of the trip.

My security agents scan the boat from the

nearby dock and a moment later are met by members of Santiago's staff. I watch in amusement as they enter into discussion. For a moment it looks a little heated, so I step out of the car while they're distracted, approaching from behind.

'Is there a problem?'

One of my guards turns to face me, his features showing consternation. 'No, ma'am. It's just a matter of logistics.'

Santiago's staff member speaks over the top of him. 'Mr del Almodóvar values his privacy and has requested your company. Alone.'

My lips twitch in amusement, even when I know I should be annoyed. After all, I've told him I don't want to draw attention to what we're doing, and that includes amongst my staff. Nonetheless, you can't make an omelette without breaking eggs and, given the level of intrusion in my life, I was probably living in a fantasy world to think I could keep things completely secret.

'I trust Mr del Almodóvar,' I say firmly, surprised to realise that it's true. I do trust him. 'Go back to the hotel and wait for me there.'

'But—'

'I mean it,' I say, but gently now, smiling to soften my command. After all, I rarely give such edicts. 'I'll be fine.'

It clearly doesn't satisfy either of them, but they take a step back, signalling tacit agreement, and I expel the breath I was holding.

A moment later, I'm walking up the gang plank of the yacht, with no idea if that's actually what it's called, my pulse running away with me at the prospect of seeing Santiago again. Excitement bursts through me.

His own staff stays on the marina.

'Hello?' I call, smiling despite the fact he hasn't appeared.

The boat begins to move and I reach out, putting my hand on the railing to steady myself, my smile growing wider as I step away from the edge look for the steering wheel. Is that even what it's called on a yacht?

Santiago is standing at the front of the boat, wearing only a pair of shorts, low-slung to reveal his toned, tanned waist, his shapely legs and strong shoulders.

Desire rushed through me.

'Is this a kidnapping?' I ask as I approach him from behind.

He casts a glance over his shoulder, his eyes locking to mine so my smile drops, the sheer heat in his look almost knocking me sideways. 'Definitely.'

A *frisson* of need runs through me. The idea

of being this man's captive is unexpectedly appealing.

He deftly manoeuvres the yacht from the marina with the ease of a man who does this regularly and, once through the barrier, he sets the control in position and turns to me properly. His fingers lift, catching a hint of my dark wig, brushing it between his forefinger and thumb.

'Do you like it?'

'I thought I would.' He lifts it from my head, nodding approval at the reappearance of my blonde hair. 'But this is better.'

My heart skips a beat.

'How did you sleep?'

'Like a log.'

'And naked?'

Heat bursts through me. I don't answer.

'I imagined you naked.' He turns back to the controls, steering the boat, with no idea what his throwaway comment does to my equilibrium. I'm knocked completely sideways.

'How was your meeting?' My voice is gravelled and uneven. I come to stand to his right, staring ahead rather than looking directly at him.

'Last night?' I prompt when he doesn't answer.

'Fine.'

Out of nowhere, a blade of jealousy assails

me, as the unpleasant thought occurs to me that he'd left me to meet another woman. Memories of the phone call where a woman's voice had been audible in the background make my breath feel hot in my lungs. My envy is based on nothing but fear—I don't know Santiago that well but I somehow trust that he's not the kind of man who would go from making love to me to being with another woman all in the same night.

I move away from him on the pretence of exploring, moving across the deck and then along a railing, ducking into the main cabin and marvelling at the space—it looks like a state-of-the-art hotel, all glossy white with plush décor, sofas and an enormous television.

I'm aware that we've stopped moving and a glance through the windows shows only ocean and, in the distance, a stunning view of the city. There are no other boats that I can see, and we're far from the land—far enough to render the buildings miniature.

'There you are.' He pulls me into his arms, kissing me hard and fast, as though he's been aching to do this all his life.

My head spins. 'Hi.' The word is just a breath in my mouth.

'I'm glad you came.'

'Well, as it turns out, I didn't have anything else to do,' I tease.

His laugh is a rumble. 'Are you hungry?'

'After that breakfast? I don't know if I'll ever eat again.'

'I'm glad you have energy.' His eyes spark with mine, his meaning clear, and I laugh——but there's an undercurrent of need pulling at me, drawing me to him, so I ache for him to kiss me again.

'Where are we?'

'Drifting in the Balearic sea.'

I breathe in the salty air, letting it touch my throat. That sense of freedom is back, taunting and tempting me. Freedom is an illusion for me, but for the next little while I can pretend.

'This boat is something else.'

'Surely you're used to such things?'

'On the contrary, I could never have something so decadent. With taxpayer money? Absolutely not.'

'Says the woman who lives in a palace?'

'That belongs to the people of Marlsdoven,' I point out.

His lips quirk as though he doesn't believe me. 'And the land I'm going to buy from you?'

The remark is jarring. I pull away from him a little, a sense of heaviness in my heart assailing me out of nowhere.

'It also belongs to my people,' I murmur. 'I'm

simply the legal custodian. Which is why I must be very careful with what happens to it.'

To my relief, he lets the subject drop. 'Hungry or not, I want to show you something.'

Curious, I allow his fingers to weave through mine so he can draw me through the yacht into a living area that also has a large kitchen, all gleaming white with high ceilings. He pulls a tray from the bench and walks towards me, gesturing towards it.

Rows of little chocolates sit waiting for attention.

'What are they?'

'A delicacy. Truffles flavoured with saffron and pistachio.'

I run my eyes over the pretty platter and, after a moment of hesitation, Santiago lifts one, bringing it to hover at my lips. 'Allow me.'

I open my mouth so he can slip the chocolate inside, the flavour exploding in my mouth dwarfed only by the sensual awareness of the man opposite, who keeps his finger pressed to my lip as I finish the confectionery.

'Well?' His eyes probe mine.

'Delicious. Savoury and sweet at the same time.'

He nods his approval. 'They are my favourite.'

He replaces the tray on the kitchen bench then nods to the deck. 'Shall we?'

I blink. 'Shall we what?' My temperature is already sky-high.

His smile shows he understands the direction of my thoughts. 'Sunbathe, of course.' His wink is that of the bad boy I know him to be, and yet I fall into step behind him. When he gestures to a row of four sunbeds lined up at the front of the yacht, I take a middle one, relaxing as the sun wraps me in warmth.

'I don't remember the last time I did this. If ever.'

'Holidayed?'

I nod. 'Most of my trips are official, and there's barely a free moment to relax. I don't mind—if I'm going to be away from home, I'd rather use the time productively. But I've almost forgotten what it's like to simply…exist.'

He reaches out and laces our fingers together. 'You're working now too. Sort of.'

'But let's not, today.' I decide on the spur of the moment, looking at him directly. 'Let's not talk about the casino or the land. I know we have to, at some point, but it will just ruin things to do so now.'

His eyes narrow and for a moment I wonder if he's going to argue but then he shrugs indolently. 'Very well, *querida*. If you wish.'

The sun lances across him, a golden blade that invites my fingers to reach out and touch.

Instead, I simply stare, my eyes drinking in the sight of him.

'You must travel often for work?' he prompts, either unaware of my shameless lusting or choosing not to acknowledge it.

I swallow past a constricted throat. 'Not that often, actually.' My eyes flick to his. 'Mainly in neighbouring Scandinavian countries, occasionally further afield. I went to Australia two years ago.'

'Did you like it?'

I nod. 'Oh, very much. I don't know if I've ever been to a country with such dramatic differences. One day I was in the tropics and the next in wineries shrouded in mist. There's snow and deserts, beaches filled with white sand and turquoise water—they put me in mind of the Mediterranean. And the people are so friendly.'

'Was it a work trip?'

'Of course.' I nod. 'And it was quick. I saw a lot, but my schedule was crammed full, so most of the "seeing" was done through the windows of my limousine.'

His lips twist for a moment, and again I have a sense that there's something he's not saying, but the look is gone again almost immediately.

'What work were you doing?'

'Studying their tourism industry. Marlsdoven is very small but very beautiful. We want more people to come and see it for themselves. Sadly, we're overshadowed by our more well-known neighbours.'

He nods thoughtfully, his eyes sparking with mine for a moment.

I sigh, his point, though not spoken, well taken. 'I suppose you think your casino will attract tourists.'

'Undoubtedly, but we aren't talking about that today.'

I turn my attention to the view, the beautiful glistening sea beyond the yacht, the warmth of the sun, the drama of the city in the distance. The famous spires of the Sagrada Familia, Gaudi's vision, reach towards the sky surrounded by a glow of terracotta, all golden and red. The contrast with the aqua colour of the ocean is almost too beautiful to bear.

'My government is focussing on transport infrastructure,' I say after a moment. 'We want to make it easy and cheap to come to Marlsdoven. A high-speed rail line is being designed at the moment, with the hope of bringing visitors directly from Amsterdam.'

He doesn't reply, and silence clouds around us, but it's a content silence, the gentle lapping of waves against the boat lulling me until my breathing slows and my eyes feel heavy.

'Why did you buy into casinos?'

The question is slumberous, and I don't look at him.

'You mean the dens of iniquity that make me my fortune?' he asks with a hint of mockery. I flick my gaze to him and my heart twists painfully in my chest. He is way too handsome. It's not fair.

'Potayto…potahtoe…' I say with a lift of my lips.

'You forget, *querida*. I made my fortune on the stock market. What is that if not a form of gambling?'

'It's not the same thing.' Though already I'm aware of my weakness here. I don't know enough about share trading to speak with authority.

'It is close to it. While there is a little more knowledge at play, mostly it's about spotting trends, often about following intuition. It's risky and fortunes can be lost in the blink of an eye. Sound familiar?'

'It's still different.'

'Why?'

'I don't know,' I say honestly. 'But it is.' Thinking about it a little more, I sit up straighter, no longer relaxed enough to drift away on a cloud of sleep. 'People don't generally wander into the stock market and throw away their life savings. For one thing, it's not easy to do—

you have to have an account or a trader who places…bids…or whatever it's called…on your behalf. When casinos are on every street corner, then every man and his dog can wander into the lobby and spin a roulette wheel.'

'Roulette wheels are not in the lobby, and we are a strictly no-animal establishment,' he drawls.

I roll my eyes and, despite the heavy direction of our conversation, find myself smiling at his quick rejoinder. 'I'm serious. The stock market is intimidating and there are barriers to people partaking. Those barriers mean most people have a level of knowledge before they open an account. A casino has no such barriers.'

'Age isn't a barrier?'

'So you have to be eighteen to gamble. Big deal.'

'It is my turn to ask a question,' he says thoughtfully. 'Why do you hate casinos so much?'

My eyes fill with light. I swallow quickly, looking away, my family's secret like a hole in my chest. 'We've discussed that.'

'You've told me you disapprove of gambling. But why?'

'Because people lose their savings. It's damaging.' My heart is racing. 'And we said we wouldn't talk about this.' I reach out, putting a hand on his knee. 'Not today.'

His eyes war with mine, the part of Santiago that wants to win, the ruthless businessman who sniffs out the advantage and mercilessly pushes it home, finding it hard to let the matter drop. But, to my surprise and relief, he does exactly that. His smile doesn't reach his eyes, but he offers one anyway.

'We will not talk about it,' he says with a clipped nod. 'But promise me this.'

I wait, my breath held.

'Come to the casino floor with me tonight. Let me show you what it's really like.'

I stiffen at the very idea. 'I toured your casino yesterday, remember?'

My voice is unintentionally icy; I hear the tone and inwardly wince.

His expression is relaxed but I feel the intensity reverberating off him in waves. 'Did you play any of the games?'

'Games?' I respond sharply, thinking only of my uncle. 'You do realise that's part of the problem? People think it's all fun and harmless but it's not. "Games" is a misnomer, if ever I heard one.'

A muscle jerks in his jaw. 'And because of your personal animosity towards gambling you are determined to keep it from your society for ever?'

'That's not possible,' I say quietly.

'No.' We're in agreement and yet I feel like the air between us is sparking with tension. Electricity fills my fingertips. 'Perhaps at some point, but not in the twenty-first century. People travel easily, play online.'

'"Play",' I say with a shake of my head.

'What would you prefer I say? Dice with danger?'

'It would be more accurate.'

'Your hatred makes no sense.'

'Not to you perhaps.'

'So explain it to me.'

I bristle, swallowing to bring back moisture to my dry mouth. 'There's no point. It hardly seems to matter. My personal feelings on the casino are by the by. I've accepted that your development will go ahead. All I care about now is making sure my country gets the utmost financial reward from the endeavour.' Again, I hear the words, and they are laced with condemnation. I wish I could control my emotions but a hatred for gambling—and an awareness of its evils—has been drummed into me for a very long time. I cannot think of my uncle or my parents without being conscious of the enormity of this betrayal.

My breath burns in my throat.

'It is not by the by to me.' His nostrils flare with the statement and for a moment my stomach swoops with something like pleasure. His interest is flattering and dangerously addictive. I quickly remind myself that it has nothing to do with me and everything to do with Santiago: he has to understand people, things, problems. It's in his nature to know everything he can about a person.

'Tell me,' I murmur. 'When you first began trading in the phantom stock-market scenario, how did you do it?'

The conversation change annoys him. I wonder if he'll brush the question aside to return to interrogating me but he doesn't. 'I researched trends. I watched carefully. I immersed myself in everything I could on the matter. Why?'

It's just as I suspected. He has to understand everything and, right now, he's trying to understand me—but only so he can turn me to his advantage. It has nothing to do with wanting to know me, or caring about me as a person.

As a child, I was winded once when I fell off a horse. I landed on my back and all the air was drummed from my body, so I lay staring up at the clear blue sky, stars dancing on the lids of my eyes. My nanny's terrified face had hovered on the periphery of my view with me unable to offer any form of reassurance for many minutes, until slowly my lungs remembered their purpose and accepted air once more. I feel that again now, without the provocation of a fall. Several realisations slam into me at once, each on their own with the power to knock my lungs to oblivion.

I want him to care about me.

I have had no one to care about me for a very long time.

I care about him.

I feel the colour drain from my face and quickly drop my face to look at my toes. In a rare tilt of the cap to vanity, I had them painted a pearly pink before coming to Barcelona. What was that if not an admission that I'd hoped my toes might be seen by this man?

'You look as though you've seen a ghost,' he murmurs. 'Do you disapprove of my techniques? Were you hoping my answer would somehow make your argument for you?'

I'm glad for the reminder of our discussion, and even more so for the lifeline he's thrown me. 'In some ways, it does.' My voice is a little hoarse. 'You are highlighting the differences between gambling and trading, though I'm not sure it matters. I wasn't the one who drew that comparison in the first instance.'

'No, it was me. Risk and reward, the story of

life. Here's another expression that is bandied about—"nothing ventured, nothing gained".'

My eyes fire to his. 'Surely it could also be, "nothing ventured, nothing lost",' I point out, my uncle heavy in my heart.

'That is a very boring way to live.'

'What you call boring, I call safe.'

'Safety from the privileged perspective of your palace is a very different consideration.'

I feel that judgement again, the same vein that had run through our first meeting and that has reared its head again here. 'You dislike the fact I'm royalty.'

His sneer shouldn't have made him more attractive, but somehow it does. 'I dislike any form of social elitism.'

'Says the man with the million-dollar yacht?'

'Bought with money I earned.'

'You don't think I earn my money?' And out of nowhere I feel rage and frustration boiling through my blood. I stand up, needing to throw my words not only at Santiago but into the sea, the sky, to have them heard on some elemental level.

'I have given my life over to my people,' I say angrily, stalking towards the yacht's railing. 'I have no privacy, no personal life, and until twenty-four hours ago I had never taken a lover. Did you know, Santiago, that you are the first man who's ever so much as kissed me? You have no idea what I have given up because I am royal. You talk about the privilege of my position without having any idea of what I have sacrificed.'

His expression gives little away, but he stands and walks towards me, his eyes raking my face, his body moving closer to mine.

'Don't you think I live every day with a horrible resentment right here——' I press my hands to my ribs '——at what is expected of me?'

'So why do it?'

My laugh is scoffing. 'What choice do I have? I have no siblings, no cousins. There is no one to take up the mantle I wear. I cannot abdicate—that choice is not for me. And, even if it were, that's not the way it's done. Not in my family, and not by me. My parents raised me to understand my responsibilities and I would never shame them, disappoint them, by turning my back on this. I am the Crown Princess of Marlsdoven and in less than a year I will become her Queen.'

'And then you will marry the man your parents chose for you,' he says quietly, and I wonder at that same sense of pain sliding through my abdomen.

'Yes.' I tilt my chin in defiant acceptance. 'These are all the things I do because I've been born to this position. So do not talk to me about privilege when your life is not hemmed in at every turn by expectations and obligations.'

It is as though a small electrical storm is raging between us, arcs of lightning threatening to incinerate me. I suck in air, but it burns in my mouth, the acrid taste of electricity palpable all the way down.

'You have been born to your position but you are the only one allowing those expectations to define you.'

I shake my head. 'You don't understand. It's not your fault; how could you?'

His eyes narrow. 'How could I? A nobody who was born in abject poverty, do you mean?'

'Please don't do that,' I snap. 'Don't make me a snob because it suits your narrative.'

'And what narrative is that?'

Our argument has clarified everything for me. I understand now the expression I see in his eyes sometimes, and why he arrived at the palace that day with a monumental chip on his shoulder. 'The one where I somehow think I'm better than you and everyone else just because I was born a royal. I don't. If I had my way, I'd abolish the whole damned idea of royalty. But to my people, it matters. The institution matters.

'It's dehumanising and grotesque. I am not a person to anyone in my life, Santiago, I am a figurehead. Can you even imagine? My face is on tea towels and mugs and postcards, sold at corner stores and airports for tourists to snap up. My parents' faces are emblazoned across those same postcards and tacky souvenir pencils. We are not people to anyone; we are property of the Marlsdoven people. That is as it is. It has always been this way, but at one point there was more actual power and far less intrusion. Now the role involves smiling at commemorative events and never putting a foot out of line lest I am accused of being ungrateful and a freeloader. That is my life. That is my so-called privilege.'

Sympathy stirs in his expression but his response is tougher than nails. 'So fight it.'

'I can't.'

'What would happen if you started to live your life as you wish? If you dated and wore jeans and spoke out about the things that matter to you? Would you be fired?'

'I can't be fired.' I shake my head. 'It's constitutionally impossible.'

'Then you would be criticised,' he says. 'And you hate the idea of that.'

I jerk my gaze away in agreement.

'But that is *your* choice. Risk and reward. You do not take the risk and so cannot enjoy the rewards.'

'I'm not at liberty—'

'You are a human being with inherent rights and the ability to choose how to live your life.'

'You just don't get it.'

'Don't I?'

'No. Until I can forget my parents, I can never forget what they expected of me.'

His eyes lance mine. 'And that's for you to be miserable?'

'I'm not miserable,' I deny, but the words lack conviction even to my own ears.

'It is for you to marry a man you've never met, who by your own admission you feel no desire for?'

'Sex isn't important.'

His laugh is sharp. 'Careful, *querida,* or I will show you exactly how false that statement is.'

His words—and the image they evoke—make my legs feel hollowed out. I fight the tug of sensual need, though it bombards me from every direction, I'm desperately clinging to my train of thought.

'The marriage agreement was formed a long time ago. It's binding.'

'And were you part of this agreement?' he prompts, with a hint of cynicism in his tone.

'I didn't know anything about it until my parents died.'

His eyes flash. 'So they never spoke of this to you?'

'I'm sure they would have,' I respond defensively. 'When I was old enough.'

'Then how do you know this is what they wanted?'

I blink at him, confused.

'You say they made this arrangement many years ago. What if their intentions changed?'

'Then they would have torn up the contract. It was kept in the family safe with all their most important documents.'

'Isn't it possible they simply forgot?'

I shake my head. 'I don't think so.'

'So you will live your life as they dictated many years ago. But this is a decision you make. You are complicit in your fate, Freja.'

'I know that. Why do you think I'm here with you?'

His eyes pierce mine.

'Rebellion.' I answer my own question. 'A taste of freedom before I return to the palace and take on all that is expected of me.'

A muscle in his jaw flexes but he says nothing. I feel his disapproval and for the first time in my life see my decisions as exactly that—decisions *I've* made.

'What would you have done? If your parents had laid out this plan for you?'

His lips tighten into a grimace. 'Run a mile in the opposite direction.' He moves closer. 'But it's a poor comparison. I am not close to my parents and generally choose to feel the opposite to them about everything.'

'Oh.' It's enough of a revelation to pull me out of my own angst. 'Why aren't you close to them?'

His shrug is a study in indifference, but I see beneath it the harsh resolution, the determination to push me away. 'Many reasons, *querida,* all of them boring.' He holds out a hand, his eyes sparking with mine. 'And I'd much rather help you rebel.'

CHAPTER EIGHT

THE SUN IS low in the sky, a golden orb blazing across the horizon spreading purple and peach colours into the heavens.

I know that we need to go back soon, that my security will be wondering where I am, worrying about me, and yet my limbs are heavy, filled with a reluctance to leave this sanctuary. If embassies are slices outside of a country's borders then this yacht is like a fragment of life existing beyond my reality. Here time has stopped and, even though I know that's not possible, I'm almost incapable of caring about the outside world right now.

'I have a question for you.'

In the kitchen, Santiago pauses, looking at me through shuttered eyes before returning to the platter he's arranging.

'Go on.' There's hesitation in his voice and I dip my head to hide a smile. He can read me like a book yet he pushes me away at every opportunity. It's frustrating and hurtful—yes, hurtful.

'You're…how old?'

Relief lightens his eyes. 'Your question is to ask my age?'

'I'm going somewhere with this,' I warn.

'I see.' He sips his beer. 'I turned thirty-one a few months back.'

I nod thoughtfully.

'And?' he prompts, lifting a wooden board off the kitchen bench and bringing it to the coffee table in front of me. The décor in the yacht is striking. Instead of the white leather and chrome I might have imagined, the interior is stylish and minimalistic, with light timber and cream fabrics. He takes a seat beside me on the lounge, so close our knees brush and, although we've spent the afternoon in bed, my pulse goes haywire at the innocent touch.

'Well, the first time we slept together…' my cheeks spread with warmth '…you said something about always taking precautions. That you don't want children.'

He dips his head once in silent agreement but there's an inherent tension to him. He's instantly wary, as though my line of questioning is the last thing he wishes to discuss.

'Why not?' I reach for an olive. It's plump,

salty and juicy, and I have to bite back a moan of pleasure as I swallow the flesh.

'You think it's strange?'

'Why are you answering my questions with a question?'

'You ask a lot of questions.'

'No, I think I've just asked one you don't want to answer.'

He weighs that up, his lips compressed in a tight line, and I wonder if he's just going to ignore me. Time drags. Tension grows inside me. Finally, he responds, the words curt. 'I have never wanted children.'

His tone leaves me in little doubt that this matter is closed, at least so far as his willingness to answer my questions. I consider pushing him, but know it would be futile. I've hit a brick wall.

'I've always known I would have to have children,' I explain. The full force of his attention is on my face, his eyes studying me intently. 'And more than one. I'm an only child and it's put a lot of pressure on me—I'm the sole surviving heir to the throne.'

'So, when you are married this will be high on your agenda?'

I nod, but the idea suddenly fills me with a drowning sensation of panic. I will need to conceive almost immediately, and that will mean having sex with my husband, a man who leaves me cold. My eyes widen as I look at Santiago and what I see on his face stills my pulse. There is a coldness in his face, a look that sends a shiver down my spine.

'And your fiancé agrees with this?'

'He's not my fiancé. I've told you.' My voice shakes a little. I take a deep breath to calm my nerves. 'And we've never discussed any of this.'

'Then what if he doesn't want children?'

'That's not an option.'

'How well do you know this man?'

'We've met a handful of times.'

'Then you know nothing about him.'

'I know that his parents—'

'And your parents were friends. But beyond this?' His disapproval is obvious, and it frustrates me now just as much as ever.

I shrug. 'I don't know if it matters.'

'That is insane.'

'Why?'

'Because you're talking about marrying the guy. Shouldn't you at least see if you're compatible?'

'Sexually?'

'*Sí,* of course, but I actually meant in any way. What if his politics differ completely to yours? What if he has a twisted sense of humour? Or wears his underpants on the outside of his clothes?'

'Like a superhero? I've always had a bit of a Lois Lane fantasy, you know.'

His eyes hold a contemplative glimmer. 'I am sure there are other ways to indulge that.'

'Oh? Such as flying off a building?'

His lips flicker in a half-smile, but he's not easily put off the conversation. 'What if you hate him?'

Anxiety trickles down my spine. 'I…won't.'

His scepticism is obvious, and makes me feel about an inch tall. 'Because your parents knew his parents?'

I swallow past a suddenly constricted throat. 'Because I *can't* hate him. I have to make it work.'

His silence speaks volumes.

'You think I'm crazy.'

'I think you obviously loved your parents very much.'

The observation is so unexpected it takes my breath away. I nod, looking away quickly.

'Losing them must have been very difficult.'

Tears threaten. I swallow quickly, then reach for a piece of cheese. 'That's an understatement.' And, even though I'm sure he knows what happened, even though I know Santiago will have done his research before coming to Marlsdoven,

I say quietly, 'Their car rolled while travelling in Africa. It was a freak accident—the first of its kind to happen to the tour company. My father died instantly, my mother two days later— just long enough for me to fly to her side and be there when she took her last breath. I'll never forget what she looked like at the end. So pale and weak. It was awful.'

He says nothing, and I'm glad.

'I always find it hard to hear from people like you, people who have their parents but choose not to be close to them. I would give everything I have for one more day with my mum and dad.'

His eyes hold mine and, even though I think he reads me easily, I have no idea what he's thinking or feeling. 'It is natural you would feel this way. You view parenthood through the veil of your own experiences.'

'What are your parents like?'

There is tension in the harsh angles of his face. He's quiet again, and I wonder if he's going to ignore me, but then he offers me one curt word.

'Different.'

'To you?'

'Yes, thank Christ.' His short laugh lacks humour.

'How so?'

He expels a sharp breath, his nostrils flaring. 'Does it matter? They're not in my life. I prefer not to think of them unless I really can't avoid it.'

I reach for another piece of cheese simply to hide my face. I'm hurt. It's such a cold rejection.

But he understands, because he sighs heavily. 'Does it matter?' he repeats, but I hear the plea in his words. He doesn't want to talk about this, but he will, if I push him.

I flick a glance at him; his face gives little away. If I didn't know him as well as I do, I would say that he's the same ruthless billionaire I first met. But deep in his eyes I see sadness, and I ache for him then.

'How about just the bullet points?' I suggest as a compromise.

He stands abruptly, moving into the kitchen and bracing his palms on the counter, looking out to sea. Guilt washes over me. I'm being selfish by asking this of him.

'I'm sorry,' I say, without moving. 'I was just trying to learn more about you. But if you really don't want to tell me…'

'My parents can tell you nothing about me,' he responds with a cool voice. 'I haven't seen them in years.'

I nod thoughtfully, looking for a way to change the subject.

To my surprise, Santiago continues, almost as

if the words are being dragged from him. 'My mother is a drug addict. Most of my childhood she was high, wasted or jonesing for her next fix. My father has been in and out of prison all his life. When he was home, he was aggressive and drunk. They fought constantly. He was abusive until I got big enough to fight back. Is this what you want to know?' His eyes lance mine. I'm incapable of responding. 'I left home when I was eighteen years old.'

I shiver at the brevity of his response—he's compressed eighteen years' worth of pain into a few spasmodic sentences but I feel the undercurrent of emotions beneath his words. 'You haven't seen them since?'

He turns to face me but looks right through me, the curl of derision on his lips reserved for his absent parents. 'If only that were true,' he drawls. 'Stories of my success landed in the national papers. They came knocking then.'

I frown, not understanding.

'For money,' he clarifies cynically. 'My mother figured I owed her after all the money she spent raising me.'

I draw in an indignant breath. It doesn't sound like his mother had much of a hand in raising him at all.

'I hope you said no,' I mutter.

'No, *querida*. I gave them money. I hoped

they'd use it to help themselves, but they spent it on drugs, parties. I only hear from them now when they want something.'

It is a throwaway comment but it clarifies something important for me. I reach for my drink, my mind analysing this tiny piece of his puzzle. Santiago was a boy who saw his parents constantly intoxicated, ignoring him, refusing to give him the love that all children crave. They let him walk away as a teenager, and only tried to see him once he had money. Their interest in him was purely mercenary.

No one has ever loved him—not in a meaningful way—and he's spent a lifetime pushing people away. He has surface-level relationships that revolve around sex because…because why? Because he's afraid? I turn to look at him and see the beautiful strength of Santiago shimmering, showing me the boy he used to be, a boy who was rejected over and over again, who lived the kind of life I can only imagine. A mother who was always wasted or looking to score drugs. A father who was either abusive or in prison. No wonder he's so messed up when it came to relationships. No wonder he doesn't want children!

I'm moving to him before I can stop myself, anguish in my heart and sorrow on my face. He stiffens, his body language reserved and laced with rejection, but I push past that because I finally understand *why* he's so determined to push me away.

I put my hand over his heart and stare into his eyes.

'Santiago, I...' But whatever I'd been about to say is constricted in my throat. My own doubts run through me, along with the reality of my life and my situation—the duties awaiting me once I leave Spain. I flash him a smile, but it feels strained. 'I really should get back to the hotel, don't you think?'

The stars twinkle overhead like diamonds in the sky and the yacht rocks from side to side, gently, beautifully, placating me into a sense of blissful relaxation.

I didn't go back to the hotel after our conversation earlier. Instead, we swam off the back of the boat. The water was warm, the sun high overhead and afterwards I was starving. We finished the platter then shared a bowl of strawberries in the hot tub, before making love right here on the deck of the yacht, the sky our only witness, heaven above me and all around me.

'You're very good at this,' I murmur, my eyes heavy.

'At what?'

'Seduction. The whole thing. Is this what it's usually like for you?'

The moonlight slices like a silver blade across his handsome face. I push up onto my elbow so I can see him better.

'I don't have a "usual",' he says after a moment. I wonder at the erratic beating of my heart. Too fast one moment, too slow the next. 'But I can say that my experience with you is unlike anything I've ever known.'

My heart speeds up way too fast. 'Oh?'

'For one thing, you are the only princess I have slept with.' He moves closer. 'And, for another, most women do not argue with me the way you do.'

My heart rolls and tumbles. Something hard is at my side again, painful and urgent. I swallow, dropping onto my back. Superficial relationships—that's what he has. And even though I now understand why, it doesn't make it any easier to cast myself—and what we're doing— in that light.

'I imagine women generally trip over themselves for your attention.'

'Something like that.' He leans over me, his eyes flicking my face. Does he see the jealousy tearing through me? 'But not you.'

'No,' I agree, my admission a whisper in the night. 'I wanted to hate you.'

'I know.' He traces my lips with the tip of his finger. 'Because of the casino?'

'The casino. Your reputation,' I say honestly. 'Everything about you is so threatening to me. I think even before I met you I knew that you were someone who could threaten the very safe walls I've built around my life.'

'Is that what I'm doing?'

Yes. Undoubtedly. But, of course, it's not really. After this, I have to go back to Marlsdoven, to my perfectly planned life, to the man I'll one day marry, to the expectations I've always borne and which have weighed me down since my parents' deaths. As for Santiago, he doesn't want to shake the walls of my life. This is just meaningless for him. A fling, nothing more.

He moves his finger to the tip of my nose, running it over the ski-jump tip.

'At that first meeting, you were full of fire,' he says, and I blush, remembering the way we'd sparked off each other.

'You were hardly Mr Congeniality yourself.'

'I never am.' He brushes aside my remark. 'But I had expected you to be calm and agreeable. I expected you to be desperate for me to sign the contract, delighted to have the land disposed of and a project like the casino undertaken. I did not anticipate, for one minute, that you would so strenuously object.'

There's something in his eyes that makes me pause, frowning. 'And that bothers you? You're disappointed?'

His features tighten. He's doing it again—looking for ways to avoid answering me.

I sigh. 'Don't worry. Forget I asked.'

He presses a finger to my lips. 'I'm used to winning. I ordinarily take great pleasure in eviscerating anyone who gets in my way.' His accent is thick, his words raw, and my nerves tingle at the picture he paints. 'I did not expect your opposition but, once I had it…'

I wait. For some reason with breath held. 'Yes?'

But he shakes his head, not finishing the thought. I don't know if he needs to. I can join the dots.

I'm his adversary in business right now, but he doesn't want to eviscerate me. He's holding back on the casino because he doesn't want to see me upset.

It's hardy a declaration of anything beyond basic courtesy—we are, after all, sleeping together—but it warms me from the inside out, regardless.

'You're different to what I expected,' he finishes with a too-casual shrug.

'Do you ever get lonely?' The question erupts before I can stop it, and only as I speak the words do I realise it's been humming inside me since we had the conversation about his parents.

'No.'

I'm glad he doesn't remind me of how busy is his social life—and by social life I mean sex life. Besides, I'm sure he's lying.

'Santiago…' I sigh, pressing a hand to his chest. 'You keep pushing me away. Is it so hard for you to be honest with me?'

'How am I not being honest?'

'Well, is there anyone in your life? Anyone who you let care about you? Anyone you care about?'

His eyes show fierce rejection of even the idea. 'My business is my life. It's all I need, *querida*.'

He sounds so certain, so confident on this score, that for a moment I wonder if I'm wrong. Perhaps my own loneliness is slanting my perception of his life. After all, I'm used to keeping almost everyone at arm's length. Claudia is probably the closest thing I have to a friend, and she works for me. Maybe I'm projecting my own feelings onto him.

Maybe I want him to tell me he *is* lonely, because in admitting that he'd be conceding he wants to make a change. And then what? Even if he were to admit he wants more in his life, it's not with me—it can't be. My own obligations prohibit that. He kisses me, and I'm glad, because the power of his kiss makes thinking almost impossible. Almost, but not quite. As he brings his body over mine, I'm acutely aware of an ache somewhere in the region of my heart.

'I love sleeping with you,' he growls in my ear, and the words send little sparks through my body. I'm flattered but afraid because, while I love sleeping with him too, there's so much more to it, and I know I can never admit that— I know he'll never feel it.

CHAPTER NINE

I'm in trouble.

I SMILE AS I send the text message, fully aware I shouldn't be so flippant. It's quite clear from the looks on my security agents' faces that they'd been about to mount an armed search for me. My disappearance was highly out of character, so I can understand their concern, but I'm not even a little sorry for it.

For the first time in my life, I've done something selfish just because I wanted to and, God, it felt good.

?

Even his reply makes me smile, because it's so business-like and to the point. I can imagine the quirk of his brow that would have accompanied it, the look of quizzical enquiry marring his symmetrical face.

Let's just say my disappearance elicited some concern.

Ah. Should I expect to be charged with kidnapping after all?

Definitely. But don't worry, I'll come see you in prison.

I should hope so.

My heart turns over in my chest. I stare at the phone, my finger hovering over the screen as I draft and redraft another message in my mind until letters are swarming incoherently through my brain. I left the yacht three hours ago and already I'm wondering when I'm going to see him again. It's just because I know I only have two more nights in Spain—and I don't want to waste a minute of them.

Are you free tonight?

His message makes my heart leap through my chest and ricochet wildly around.

What have you got in mind?

A surprise. Meet me on the roof at eight.

The roof?

I'll send a key to your room.

I was joking about the whole Lois Lane jumping off a building thing.

And I'm definitely no Superman.

At least, you wear your jocks inside your trousers.

Most of the time.

I laugh, placing my phone on the table. Half an hour later, one of my security guards knocks on the door, warily handing me an envelope. I rip it open, breaths coming hard and fast, and read it in front of him. It's clear and concise instructions, written in Santiago's dark, confident writing, directing me to a private lift and a roof-top helipad, as well as a key card to activate the lift.

'I'll be going out tonight,' I say without looking at the guard, my pulse a tsunami. 'Don't wait up.'

The lights of Barcelona twinkle way below us. I stare down at the vista with true pleasure and a light heart. Wherever we're going, I don't care. In this moment, I am carefree and happy.

'I feel like all the world's a tiny little snow globe.'

'And you are what? An eagle?' His accented voice crackles over the helicopter earpieces. Any answer dies on my lips when I turn to see the expert ease with which he controls the instruments. My mouth goes dry. His sleeves are pushed up to reveal his tanned forearms, the snake tattoo drawing my gaze. There is something incredibly hot about the way he commands this expensive, powerful piece of equipment.

'Where did you learn to fly?' I ask instead.

'Around the time I bought my first jet.'

My eyes are round like saucers. 'You have more than one aircraft?'

'I have one jet now, but over the years I've owned several.'

My lips form a silent 'O' of surprise or admiration.

'It seemed to make sense to me to learn how to fly, seeing as I would be trusting my life to pilots on so many occasions.'

I twist my mouth to the side, the evidence of his obsessive control obvious in the statement. 'Do you fly your own jets too?'

'Not often. From time to time, I serve as copilot, but it's much more comfortable in the cabin.'

I don't know why but all roads with Santiago lead back to bed, and the innocuous comment makes me think of him in the bedroom of a private plane: luxurious silk sheets, mood lighting, him handsome, naked, powerful... I turn my eyes back to the view. I'm very high yet it feels much safer to look down than to stare at the man beside me.

The pressure between us builds so that with every moment that passes all I'm aware of is him, his closeness, the proximity overwhelming me. It's a relief when the helicopter starts to descend over a significantly darker patch of land. There are still lights, but far fewer. His control is expert; I gather he knows the way very well.

'You're a nervous flyer?' he asks after touching down, mistaking my tension for something else altogether.

'Not really.'

'Then you are nervous to be here with me?'

I shake my head. 'Just...a little overwhelmed, I think.'

His brows lift and then he smiles, that rare, beautiful, soul-splitting smile.

'Don't be. This is just one night out of our lives, Freja. Nothing more.'

I love it that he uses my name. My skin lifts

and, when he opens the door of the helicopter, the warm breeze rushes past me, cementing his words in my mind. *It's just one night, nothing more.*

'I figured you were right about the restaurants in Barcelona—far too likely you would be seen in a city like that. But here in Aliz it is quieter.'

Nonetheless, I lift a hand to my dark wig, glad I'd thought to wear it.

'Yes, the disguise is still good, if only because I find it impossibly sexy.' His eyes twitch at the corners and I know he's teasing me. I punch his arm playfully as we stroll slowly towards a string of restaurants lined up along a cobbled path. The walk is part of the pleasure. It is a weekend and, despite his promise that this town would be quiet, the restaurants are busy, a gentle din reaching us on the street as we go.

'Aliz is famous for its seafood,' he explains as we walk. 'People come from all around to enjoy what these places have to offer.'

'And you come here often?'

'Often enough to know which restaurant is best,' he responds with another heart-stopping smile, before gesturing towards a restaurant at our side.

The frontage is made of glass, with awnings over the top, so that in the daytime I imagine the restaurant to be filled with *al fresco* diners, sunlight filtering onto them. Now the restaurant is dressed for the evening, with candles on the table-tops and a jazzy soundtrack playing.

'Santiago!' He's greeted by the *maître d'* like an old friend returning. 'It is good to see you again.'

'Enrique.' He nods, and to my surprise they embrace, before he gestures to me. 'This is a friend of mine.' His lips twitch. 'Lois.'

I lift a brow, the alias he's chosen for me causing my heart to jackhammer against my ribs. I miss only two beats before extending my own hand to Enrique. 'Pleasure.' He lifts it to his lips but, although he is also handsome, I feel nothing. Just like before. Any time in my life that I've met a man, I've never felt so much as a flicker of my pulse. But with Santiago it's as though that's all I'm capable of feeling—totally overrun by emotions and need.

He leads us to a table at the back of the restaurant. A large indoor fig with glossy green leaves partially conceals the table from view, and for added protection I take the seat against the wall, because it obscures me completely from other diners.

'Would you like to see a menu?' Santiago asks as we take our seats.

'I'm no expert at eating in restaurants, but isn't that customary?'

'I generally rely on Enrique to bring me what's best.'

It speaks volumes, given what a control freak he is. 'Then I'm sure that will be fine.'

'Is there anything you don't eat?'

His attention to detail makes me feel like the most special person in the world. Danger signs flash. That's not what this is. It's not what he wants and it's impossible for me to want it. Impossible for me to have it. I can't look beyond this slice of time.

'Lois?'

I realise he's waiting for my answer so I shake my head softly and he conveys this to Enrique in Spanish; then, we are alone.

'How did you find this place?'

'I first came here many years ago. I was looking at developing a hotel on the foreshore, just over there.' He points to a window and I lean forward, following the direction of his finger. It's dark outside, just the faint glow of pale streetlights showing the edge of the road. A beach lies beyond—we walked beside it as we arrived. The moon is shining brightly tonight, casting a silver skein across the ancient, rumbling sea.

'But you didn't?'

A waiter arrives with a bottle of champagne. He stands at the table as he removes the foil and pops the top, then tilts the glasses individually to fill them.

Both of us alone again, I run my finger over the stem of my wine glass, watching Santiago. He lifts his glass, silently gesturing to mine. I mimic the gesture, then sip. The drink is ice-cold with the slightest fizz. It tickles my tongue and dances all the way down. I close my eyes to enjoy the flavour and, when I open them again, Santiago is staring at me. My mouth goes dry despite the dousing of champagne. I blink, self-conscious and bursting with sensation.

'No.' The word is gruff and it takes me a moment to remember that we were talking about his hotel development.

'Why not?'

'In the end, it wasn't suitable.'

Now, *that's* interesting. 'No?' I sip my champagne, attempting to appear casual.

'Part of the charm of this town is that it's largely inaccessible. This means the number of tourists is limited. I realised that, in building a hotel to capitalise on the area's appeal, I'd be destroying it.'

My jaw drops. 'So you pulled out of a financially lucrative deal because it was the right thing to do?'

'It is entirely different to the Marlsdoven casino.'

I shudder to hear it described this way. 'Why?'

He leans forward and places his hand over mine. 'For one thing, the casino will be in a major European city. For another, the hotel here would not have remained lucrative once it had taken away the quaint appeal of a tiny coastal village. I feared making the coastline into a theme park—there is long-term damage in that.'

'Not a good bet?' I prompt.

His eyes glitter darkly when they meet mine. 'Exactly. The odds were not in my favour. Whereas market research shows that the scope for a casino in Marlsdoven is enormous. Believe it or not, your population responded very favourably to the prospect, in the surveys I commissioned. Additionally, thirty-five per cent of travellers returning to Marlsdoven reported wanting a visit to a casino at some point during their trip.'

I close my eyes, a wave of nausea passing through me as I force myself to accept this reality. I already knew it was all but a done deal, but hearing these facts just show me how futile it is to keep fighting him on this.

'Why do you hate the concept so much?'

I swallow, bitterness making my throat thicken. 'I've told you—'

'Yes, you've told me,' he interrupts, but pauses as another waiter appears with a plate of food. The fragrance is unmistakably saffron. When he goes, Santiago continues. 'You've told me that you despise gambling, but you haven't told me why. And I can tell there is more to it. This is personal for you. Deeply personal.'

I stare at my hands. 'Why do you say that?'

'Because your skin grows pale whenever I bring up the casino. You look as though you've seen a ghost. This is not just business, nor is it a maternal desire to protect your citizens from the big, bad wolf of gambling. So what is it, Princesa?'

My heart stammers. I shake my head, the demurral meaningless in the face of his question. Why not tell him the truth? It is a secret I've protected all my life, which my parents valued, but I don't doubt I can trust Santiago with it.

'My uncle was a gambling addict,' I say softly, toying with the champagne flute. 'He hid it for many years. He travelled abroad, starting with poker before progressing to the casinos of Europe, where his bets grew increasingly enormous—I think in an effort to recoup some of his losses. He had a generous trust fund but he burned through it in eighteen months. His annual income from our family estates was also exceptional, but he borrowed against his share, mortgaging himself over and over until he was tied up in knots and in debt to less than savoury money lenders.'

I take a gulp of champagne, needing the liquid but also the artificial relaxation. Santiago is quiet, waiting for me to continue, and to my surprise I do. After not discussing Richard for many, many years, it feels important to speak about him. Or maybe it's just that Santiago has a unique power over me...that with him I want to be completely honest about everything.

'I think he always struggled with being the second-born son. Nothing was expected of him. He was never spoken of, never valued as more than a contingency plan if something happened to dad. He had a lot of money and fame, but no purpose. No value. And so many limitations.'

'And so he started gambling,' Santiago murmurs sympathetically.

I nod. 'My father blamed himself. He was busy with his obligations and family. They grew apart but dad always thought my uncle was happy—just living life with the kind of freedom my father would never know. If anything, I think he envied Richard a little.' I sigh.

'How did he find out the truth?'

'My uncle committed suicide.' I say the words robotically.

Santiago's brows knit closer together, his surprise evident.

I grimace. 'Nobody knew,' I explain. 'At the time, it was reported that he died after a long battle with an illness. And that's not a lie,' I hasten to add. 'Gambling addiction is exactly that.'

He dips his head in acknowledgement.

'He left a note. It revealed the extent of his losses. He felt helpless. He was in a cycle of forever trying to dig himself out of trouble. He would hope for one more win, that that would be enough to start making repayments.' I shake my head sadly. 'My father felt incredibly guilty. He had money; he could have helped. But my uncle was too ashamed to ask.'

Silence falls between us.

'I'm sorry for your loss.' Santiago's voice is carefully mute of emotion, so I don't know if the story has had any impact on him.

'Thank you.' I sip my champagne. The noise of the restaurant swirls around us, but I barely hear it.

'Your family must have been devastated.'

'Yes. He hid his addiction so well, none of us had any idea until it was too late. Per Richard's wishes, the truth surrounding his death was never revealed.'

More silence, softened by reflectiveness.

'How old were you?'

'Eleven.' I close my eyes against a wave of memory. 'It killed a part of my father, you know? He loved his brother, had always felt protective of him, and losing him like that... I know he blamed himself.'

'That's futile.'

'Perhaps. But it's also unavoidable.' I offer a tight smile. 'He was different after that. My father became obsessed with duty and responsibility, with making sure I understood the importance of our role to the kingdom. I used to think when he was lecturing me that he was imagining his brother in my place, saying the things he wished he could have said to Richard.'

Santiago's expression is analytical, his eyes scanning my face. 'And you wanted to please your father,' he murmurs eventually.

I lift one shoulder in defiant acceptance of that.

'You want to please him still,' Santiago presses and, even though it's true, I feel as though it's a criticism.

'I want to make him proud,' I say eventually.

'And how do you do that, Freja? What do you need to do?'

'That's easy,' I respond tightly. 'I do exactly what I'm meant to do. What I was born to do.'

'And never deviate from what's expected of you?'

I press my teeth into my lower lip. 'No,' I agree after a moment. 'Never.' I don't know why, but admitting that aloud feels a little like cutting off something important. I turn away, but he draws my attention back.

'Freja...' he says gently, lacing our fingers together. I stare at the contrast in our skin, his dark, mine fair, the juxtaposition enchanting. 'You say your uncle grew up second best, knowing he was second best. And you are right. Gambling is an addiction. For some people it fills a void. I just wonder that, if it weren't gambling, your uncle might have relied on another crutch. Alcohol, drugs. Both of which are equally harmful.'

I lift my gaze to his, thinking of his own experience with substance abuse, parents who'd been either high or drunk his entire childhood.

'He gambled,' Santiago continues. 'But I do not know if it necessarily follows that gambling is inherently bad.'

I drop my eyes back to our hands, staring at them. 'It killed him.'

His lack of response speaks volumes, and I don't entirely disagree with him. My uncle wasn't happy. He was looking to fill a void and he found his way to gambling. The initial high of winning made him feel good, possibly for the first time in his life. Maybe if he'd tried drugs or got into binge drinking it would have been the same.

'After the funeral, I remember my father saying that gambling is the scourge of the world… that for all that it's been around since time immemorial it should be banished, and that if he had his way it would be. He had no power over the world, but at least in Marlsdoven he could make sure the country was never touched by such a harmful practice.' My voice shakes a little. I reach for my fork, pressing it into the rice on my plate. Steam billows towards me. 'I didn't think about those words again until you made your offer.'

'And your first instinct was to reject the proposal.'

My lips tighten into something like the ghost of a smile. 'I don't really have that power. Perhaps if I asked the Prime Minister… But without an alternative that is just as beneficial to our economy…?' I shake my head sadly. 'I'm aware that I have a bias here. I know what I want is unreasonable.'

'But, if there is to be casino in Marlsdoven, you need it to be on your terms.'

My eyes widen as they lift to his. I nod. 'It has to be worth it. I don't know how I can make peace with what I owe my father, my uncle, if I don't at least try to fight this.'

He reaches for his glass and has a drink without relinquishing my hand. 'Two years ago, when I first started looking to put a casino in Marlsdoven, your government provided me with a list of land options. I chose this site because of the historic nature of the land as well as its primacy within the city––on the river bank, with easy access to the CBD. I am as convinced now as I was then that this will be the best place for the project.'

He's right. The land is ripe for development.

'Your government offered me the land,' he repeats. 'Did you know that?'

I nod. 'Every year we discuss which areas might be used and for what purpose. There has long been talk of urbanising that section of the city.'

He considers that a moment, taking a bite of his own meal. I follow suit, tasting delicate spices and butter in the rice. 'You would prefer a different kind of development.'

'Yes.'

'Such as?'

My first instinct is to tell him I've never really thought about it, but that's a lie. 'I always hoped it could be turned into a culture and arts precinct. Museums, galleries, a new theatre for ballet. Even a stadium for sporting events. I hoped we could celebrate the rich history of our arts, but the funding just isn't there.' I expel a soft sigh. 'The previous government badly mismanaged the budget and, as a result, our country's finances are in need of conservative management. It isn't the time to be investing billions of euros into a culture precinct, even though I think it would be incredibly beautiful and a great addition to our country.'

'And it would make your parents proud.'

My eyes ping to his and I nod jerkily. 'Yes.'

'Whereas, by allowing this casino to be built, you feel that you're betraying them.'

I flutter my eyes closed. 'I am betraying them. But it can't be helped.' I try to smile. 'I'm old enough to know when I'm fighting a losing battle, Santiago. I suppose the best thing to do now is focus on the positives of your development.'

I can see how unsatisfied he is with that, but he lets the conversation drop, squeezing my hand once before releasing it.

'How is your entrée?'

'Delicious,' I murmur, though I barely taste it. The conversation has filled me with emotional ambivalence. I change the subject awkwardly. 'Casinos are only a part of your business, aren't they?'

For a moment I feel as though he's going to return to our earlier discussion but then he begins to explain that, while casinos were how he first built his fortune, he's since diversified into a wide array of interests—from hedge funds to tech companies to boutique hotels and banks. He has fingers in many pies.

The food is perfect, and as our conversation moves away from the matter of the casino he wishes to build I am blissfully content. By the time we leave, the restaurant is empty.

'Oh, my goodness, I didn't realise how late it is. I'm sorry we kept you,' I apologise to Enrique.

He smiles warmly. 'It is no problem. We are always here anyway.'

Santiago embraces him once more, in the Spanish style, then loops an arm low around my waist, guiding me into the night air. In the distance I catch the gleam of his helicopter, and by unspoken yet mutual agreement we slow down, neither of us in a rush to reach it too soon.

'Thank you for bringing me here. I've had a wonderful night. I don't want it to end.' I laugh shakily.

He stops walking altogether then, turning me to face him. For the briefest moment, he is stricken, as though fighting a war within himself. He stares down at me, through me, inside me, and then expels a soft, slow breath. He lifts a hand, tucking the brown hair of my wig behind my ear.

'No?'

I shake my head, incapable of speech.

His eyes soften and I have the distinct impression he's surrendering to something he wishes he could fight. 'Then it doesn't have to, Princesa.'

CHAPTER TEN

DAWN LIGHT SHIFTS across the bed and I reach for Santiago instinctively, my fingertips brushing the sheets in search of him. But he's not there, of course. I have no concept of what time he left, or if he tried to wake me to say goodbye, I only feel a sense of incompleteness that he's not here.

It jolts me awake, so I stare at the view revealed by my window of the sun cresting over the city, and the glistening ocean, and wonder at how he's become so important to me in such a short space of time. What happened to a secret, sexy fling? A bit of fun before I go home and pick up the mantle of my responsibilities, finally becoming Queen of Marlsdoven, and all that entails?

Except he is fun, too, even as I recognise he's become something…more…something difficult to characterise. I smile as I shower, remembering the night we shared, the way he kissed me, touched me so reverently, as though he were worshipping me…as though I completed him. Of course I don't—that's just me trying to make sense of such an intimate physical act, of the way it feels when we're together. So right.

A frown is on my face as I get ready, choosing a sunny dress and sandals for my last day in Barcelona. The thought is at the edge of my mind all day, an awareness of time racing towards a finish line I no longer want to reach. What if I were to extend my trip?

Except I can't. There's a state dinner tomorrow night. That's the reason I booked my visit for these dates. I can't miss it. Not even for this.

No, I have to leave as originally planned, and then that will be the end of this.

It's late in the afternoon when my phone buzzes.

Are you free for dinner?

I roll my eyes, a smile lifting the corners of my mouth.

Who with?

Funny! I'll be back in Barcelona around six p.m. Okay?

My heart notches up a gear. Okay? It's better than okay. It's at least two hours earlier than I had expected him for dinner.

Sure. See you then.

He arrives five minutes early, carrying a large brown paper bag, and my heart races at the sight of him. He's wearing jeans and a button-down shirt with the sleeves pushed up to reveal his forearm tattoos. His skin is a golden brown, his hair pushed back from his face so the intensity of his eyes is all the more obvious. My nerves go into overdrive.

He kisses me on the cheek and my pulse throbs; it's such a normal gesture, as if we're two people who are dating, as though this isn't the last night we'll see each other. I look away, blinking rapidly to clear the thought. This isn't the time to think about that.

'What's in the bag?' I ask, lifting up to peek in the top.

'Dinner.' He lowers it to reveal a bushy green celery top and some bulbs of garlic. 'Or it soon will be.'

My brows lift in surprise. 'You're cooking?'

He sends me a sardonic look. 'That surprises you?'

'Well, obviously!' I laugh. 'I don't think I can picture you in an apron.'

'I cook shirtless.' Even though it's obviously a joke, my breath bursts out of my lungs.

He doesn't cook shirtless, but he cooks well, as though he's often done. I watch, mesmerised, sipping wine and making conversation which, he's informed me, is my job for the evening. I don't drink much, though, just a few small sips, because I want to remember every detail just as it happened without any filter over the top.

When I take a bite of the paella he makes, my lips part on a moan of appreciation. 'This is amazing.' Saffron, olives and tomato all combine to give the dish a richness that is full-bodied yet not overpowering.

He dips his head. 'I'm glad you like it.'

'How did you learn to make this?'

'It's not rocket science.'

'I just presumed you're someone who eats out every night. I had no idea you were secretly a culinary whiz.'

He grins as he lifts a fork to his mouth. 'Paella is easy.'

'I don't believe you.' I take another bite, closing my eyes as the flavours run through me. 'How did you learn?'

'Not from my mother,' he quips with a half-smile.

Sympathy stirs through me.

'My first apartment was just above a market. I used to walk past in the evenings and see the tables groaning with fresh produce—seafood, meat, vegetables, cheeses. I began to experiment. I would try to recreate meals I'd eaten at restaurants—most were deceptively simple— and I found I enjoyed it.'

'Like you do wine making,' I say, lifting the glass.

'*Precisamente*. It's a pleasure to create something exactly to your taste, to experiment until you have it just right.'

I nod thoughtfully.

'Do you cook?'

I grimace. 'No. I can't even make toast.'

He laughs, a rich sound that makes my stomach loop.

'You should learn,' he says after a beat. 'I think you'd enjoy it.'

'Oh? Why is that?'

He reaches across the table, lacing our fingers together. 'Cooking is an act of meditation and control. It's very satisfying. Besides, you need hobbies.' He winks then, but my heart lurches. Santiago is the first person in my life to see me as a woman, to want to encourage me to be more than my title and expectations. His ability to see many facets of my being is addictive and comforting. I feel fully formed when I'm with him, more human than royal, just an ordinary woman with the potential to be and do anything I wish.

I don't want the night to end.

I don't want to leave here.

And yet I know I must. Even without my father's voice and expectations constantly guiding my decision-making process, I understand what's expected of me.

I attempt to smile, pulling my hand away, and focus on the view beyond us. The waves roll towards the shore, towards this great, ancient city, just as they always have done. They'll continue rolling tomorrow, and the next day, when I'm no longer here to see them, just as Santiago will continue with his life once I'm gone.

I don't know if I'll ever be the same, though.

'What time is your flight?'

His finger traces invisible patterns over my bare flesh, his touch possessive and natural, as though he has every right to touch me whenever and however he wishes; as though my body belongs to him, and his to me. Despite my wish for time to stand still, my last day has arrived.

'Eleven.'

His finger pauses in its progress for a moment before re-starting the lazy exploration, charting across my stomach, towards my hip then back to circle my belly button. 'So early.'

'I have a state dinner at the palace tonight.' It was the constraint I'd had to work around when booking this trip. All my other engagements had been easy to cancel, but not this one.

'Back to being a princess?'

'I never really stopped,' I say with a lift of my shoulder.

'Yes, you did. For these last few days, you've simply been Freja.'

After my parents died, my life became the furthest from private it's ever been. My country was obsessed with how I was coping and, though their interest in me came from a good place, it was hard to bear. In order to cope with the burden I saw a therapist, and she told me to find one good thing every day and focus on that, to hold it tight to my chest in moments of panic and be grateful. Gratitude would save the day every time.

The idea of leaving Spain and Santiago stirs that same panic inside me, erupting out of nowhere and rising towards me like a dusk tide, so I grab hold of my gratitude. What I've experienced with this man is something I will always cherish. Even if leaving him is going to be so much harder than I'd anticipated.

And as for Santiago? Will he think of me

when this ends? Or simply move on to the next woman who catches his eye? Ice chips through me and, like a glutton for punishment, I hear myself ask, 'I suppose you'll have forgotten all about me by nightfall?'

His features are mocking, reminding me of the first time we met. He is such a contradiction; *we* are a contradiction. I feel simultaneously closer to him than I ever have another soul, but at the same time he's a constant enigma.

'You think you're so forgettable? You're the only princess I've ever slept with.'

I don't know what I want him to say; not that. 'Still just another woman in a long line of women.'

'And that bothers you?'

I feel trapped, and I don't even know why. I'm not sure why I brought this up, nor why I sound as though he's betrayed me in some way. We both knew what this was. And we both know why our relationship can never go beyond this. I have expectations on me, expectations I've carried all my life—how I'll live my life, who I'll spend it with. Marriage to a prince, children… sensible, traditional. A casual fling with a man like this would be a disgrace; my parents raised me to respect my duties, to honour the requirements of my role. This is way outside of that.

But it's okay, because it's temporary, and no one will ever find out. That's the way it has to be.

So why does it feel like I want more from him? Some kind of pledge that I mean something, when I know I don't...

'I have never lied to you about my past,' he says quietly, pressing a finger to my chin, angling my face to his. Until that moment, I hadn't realised I'd been avoiding his eyes.

'I know that.' I brush aside his comment.

'Sex is a wonderful experience to share with someone.' His voice caresses me as his words turn my heart to ice. 'I've enjoyed sharing it with you. I will always feel honoured to have been your first.'

But not my last. The words he hasn't spoken hammer through me, and I feel physically ill. Out of nowhere, a desperate sense of nausea assails me. The idea of another man ever making love to me makes my heart twist painfully.

'And, after I'm gone, I'll see photos of you in the press, with all the women you share this experience with.' Despite my best intentions, the words are hollowed out. Bitterness is recognisable in the clipped remark.

'And I will see photos of your wedding,' he reminds me, but it's simply a response rather than a complaint. His words are robbed of emotion, flat, spoken with the calm delivery of someone simply making a point.

'Yes, my wedding,' I murmur throatily, trying to remind myself of the importance of my engagement, the wedding my parents planned for something I've always accepted as a necessity. 'I wonder if I'll feel differently about Heydar now.'

Santiago's eyes narrow, his lips tight as he waits for me to elaborate.

'I've never felt anything for him before, but maybe that's because I had no experience with men. Perhaps it will be different now that I understand things more. Maybe.'

I truly wonder if this is the case, but even as I say the words I'm aware I'm seeking to provoke a reaction from Santiago. I want to make him jealous because *I* am jealous. I'm jealous of him and his freedom, and I'm jealous as hell of the women who'll come after me. The women who will get to kiss him and make love to him and feel like the centre of his universe. I want to freeze time and hold on to this moment, never letting the world intrude, pushing reality away for ever more.

'You will find out when you are married. I hope the gamble pays off.'

I lift my shoulder in a slight shrug. 'I'll find out tonight, actually.'

His face remains the same, but his eyes darken, and they bore into me with the intensity of a jet engine.

'At the state dinner,' I explain. 'Heydar's on the guest list.'

'I see.'

I can't discern jealousy. It's clear that he doesn't like the idea but, at the same time, it might just be the whole concept of an arranged marriage he's opposed to. I don't know. Frustration gnaws through me.

'And so your hope is that, now you are sexually awakened, you'll desire this man you've agreed to marry?'

'I didn't agree.'

His smirk is mocking. 'You intend to go through with it, do you not?'

'Well, yes.'

'Then you have agreed.'

'I just haven't gone against my parents' wishes,' I say. 'It's a nuanced difference.'

His response is curt, the words whipping the edges of the room. 'That results in the same thing.'

'Yes.'

'And what if you feel nothing for him tonight?'

'It won't make any difference.'

His eyes flash to mine.

'What?' I demand, wondering at the fire in my belly. 'What does it matter?'

'It doesn't,' he insists, but his voice is not mute of emotion now. I hear disapproval in every syllable, and something else too—something a lot like anger.

'Then why are you reacting like this? Why are you cross with me?'

His features show contempt. I shiver.

'What if you see him tonight and suddenly find there is chemistry between the two of you, *querida*?'

I don't know what he wants me to say. The idea disgusts me. I know that I likely won't feel anything more for Heydar that I have before. I know I won't feel anything for any man that equates to what I've shared with Santiago. I tilt my face away from his, looking towards the window.

'Then I guess that's good,' I lie, mumbling the words.

He curses in his native tongue, and I jerk my face back to his, surprised by the outburst.

'You would actually go from my bed to his?'

'Hang on a second—you're the one who was just extolling the virtues of sex and sharing sex with different partners.'

'And you're the one who is seeing her fiancé tonight, while naked beneath me.'

'He's not my fiancé,' I contradict.

'That is semantics,' he dismisses. 'You intend to marry the man. You're seeing him tonight and hoping that you feel attracted to him.'

'And what? You're jealous?'

'No,' he denies swiftly.

My breath is coming in little fits. I move my head to the side in an attempt to find sanity, then look back at him. 'I didn't mean to suggest…'

'Yes, you did.' His eyes challenge mine, so I find it hard to breathe. Guilt and shame at my childish behaviour heat my cheeks.

'I just…wish I felt for him what I do for you. That would be far more convenient,' I correct quietly.

'Because he is a suitable husband?' Santiago responds in a tone that is so quiet it roars.

My heart stammers. We stare at each other, the air between us sparking with the power of a thousand lightning bolts.

'Yes,' I say eventually. 'Because he will be my husband.'

His nostrils flare as he expels a breath. 'Tell me, Princesa, what about this man makes him suitable?'

'I… Everything.'

'By your own admission, you hardly know him.'

'I know enough.'

His eyes narrow. 'He is royal; is that your sole criterion?'

His vehemence surprises me. But hadn't I goaded him to this? Hadn't I wanted to make him jealous? It was a petty manoeuvre, to push him to reveal some kind of feeling for me—even a dark one, like envy.

'Forget I brought it up,' I say with the appearance of calm, remembering that I am a princess and I have been taught not to lose my temper. Or at least not to show that I'm losing it.

He shifts his body weight, one hand caressing my cheek. 'Do you want me to say I hate the idea?'

I blink my eyes closed, pleasure briefly feathering my heart.

'I do,' he concedes after a beat. 'I'm a regular, red-blooded man. I wouldn't be human if I didn't have some reservations about a woman I'm sleeping with moving on so quickly. Is that what you want to hear?'

Not even close. He's not jealous, he's possessive, driven by ego—there's a vital difference there.

'That seems like a double standard,' I say unevenly.

He presses a finger to my lips. 'In all this time, you are the only one who has brought others into this. You talk about the women I've slept with and the man you will marry. You say to me that you hope our relationship will make you more likely to desire him and you ask about the women I will see when you return to Marlsdoven. There are realities beyond what we share, but I am not the one making us face them.'

I flinch at his summary of the situation. Everything is so messy, and I *hate* mess.

'We have to face them, though,' I say simply, my throat thick. 'I'm marrying Heydar. Not tonight, not tomorrow, but in a few months, after my coronation. And I will never be able to see you again.'

He wouldn't want to see me again anyway. If he did he'd fight for me, of that I'm certain. Santiago is not the kind of man to lose anything or anyone he values. I mean nothing to him, and, the sooner I accept that deep in my heart, the better. It will never hurt less, but at least the knowledge will save me from making a fool of myself.

A muscle jerks at the base of his jaw, and then he kisses me hard, his lips claiming mine. It's as though he can't find the words to respond to me, so he's seeking to reply bodily, tormenting me with a desire that's eating me alive.

His kiss stirs something deep in my chest. A reality I probably already know. A sharp, dangerous knowledge that I don't want to keep hold of. I push it away resolutely, returning his kiss with all the desperation I feel—a desperation born from the fact I am leaving Spain within hours and, for the good of everyone, can never see this man again.

As pleasure floods my body, reality breaks my heart.

CHAPTER ELEVEN

HE'S QUIET BUT I don't want to read anything into that. Whatever question his silence raises, I already have the answer.

I'm leaving soon, and that will be the end of us. He doesn't look at me as he drinks his coffee, concentrating instead on the newspaper in front of him. I watch him read, marvelling at this small, ordinary action, and am struck by something unusual.

My parents used to do this.

How many mornings did I walk into the dining room to find my father reading the paper, mother opposite him? It is the most ordinary reflection of every day domesticity, and sharing it with Santiago now makes me anxious, because it's such a lie. I know I'm reading too much into it. I stand uneasily, moving towards the window. Across the room, my small suitcase is packed, stuffed with all the things I brought. Clothes that will remind me of Santiago for ever. The cap sits on top, ready for me to resume my disguise.

'We haven't talked about the casino,' I say, glancing at my wristwatch at the same time.

He lifts his gaze to my face and my heart stops beating. The golden light from behind me frames him until he shimmers. I ache for him but I know that can't happen. Like ripping off a sticking plaster, I have to go.

'We can discuss it over email,' he says quietly. 'But I see nothing in your requests that is… unreasonable.'

My eyes sweep shut. He's going to agree to my terms… Because he thinks they're fair or because we've slept together? Uneasiness grows. 'Thank you.'

The rustling of paper draws my attention back to him. He stands, walking towards me. 'I'll drive you to the airport.'

I anticipated this suggestion and have my response ready. 'I want to take a taxi. I've never done that before.'

His eyes war with mine, a challenge in their depths. 'Then I'll come with you.'

I hadn't anticipated that response, but I demur easily enough. 'It's too risky; too many people… my security guards. I'd rather say goodbye to you here. Privately.'

I wonder if he's going to overrule me, as he

did with the trip here, but after a moment he nods. 'Fine.' He rakes his fingers through his thick, dark hair and I wonder if he's experiencing a similar maelstrom of emotions as I am.

I've never been with a man before. I have no experience of any of this, particularly not with saying 'goodbye', but I have bags of history when it comes to knowing what people expect of me.

This should be light-hearted. Nothing about what we've done was ever going to be serious. We both knew that coming into it. I force a bright smile to my face. 'I've had a lot of fun with you,' I say, wondering how it became so much more meaningful than just 'fun'.

'I'm glad.' He doesn't match my smile. His hand, when it cups my cheek, is gentle. 'Try to remember what you deserve, Princesa.'

Hope briefly lifts my heart. 'And what's that?'

'More than an arranged marriage.'

On this, I know we'll never see eye to eye. There's no point discussing it further. Besides, I'm starting to worry that if we don't wrap this up quickly I might do something truly embarrassing, like crying, or begging him for one more night.

'I really have to get back.'

'Of course. Your state dinner,' he says with

only the faintest hint of emotion darkening the comment.

I nod slowly.

He drops his head but, instead of the passionate kiss I crave, I receive a chaste goodbye peck on each cheek, and then he drops my hands and takes a step backwards. 'Take care of yourself, Freja.'

I watch him walk towards the door. Every inch of me wants to run after him, but I don't. I stand exactly where I am, already feeling the heavy gravitational pull of my real life and the future that awaits me.

It turns out sleeping with Santiago changed many things about me, but not this. I still feel nothing for my future husband. He is handsome and polite, well-spoken, and there's every indication he's well-read and well-educated, but if anything the idea of our marriage leaves me short of breath—in the worst possible way. I feel like my head is being pushed under water; I'm suffocating. I speak to him for longer tonight than I have before, trying to find common ground or some kind of spark, trying to find something with which to connect with him.

There's nothing.

'We should meet privately, another time, to discuss our parents' machinations,' he says, wiggling his eyebrows as though it's all some big joke. He doesn't know my heart is breaking. I'm very good at concealing such things.

'Do you want to pretend it never happened?' I ask with what I hope seems like humour, hoping he'll agree.

'I don't think that's possible. My parents would be devastated.' His eyes scan my face. 'Would you prefer to forget it, Freja?'

Hearing him say my name angers me. Not because I care about ceremony—I don't, generally—but it's an intimacy I like sharing with Santiago alone.

'I… My parents…'

He nods sympathetically. 'My parents have explained how much it meant to yours. Our marriage was their greatest wish. So let's have dinner some time between now and Christmas. We can go over the details then. Perhaps we should go away together for a weekend, get to know one another in a more private way?'

He is everything amenable and yet disgust threatens to swallow me. I nod, because I don't trust myself to respond, and excuse myself a moment later.

It's a relief when the dinner ends and I can return to my apartment, pushing Heydar from my mind gratefully and replacing him with Santiago. I lie in my bed, altered for ever by the nights spent in Barcelona, wondering what he's doing now.

I could text him, but to what end?

We shared something special—at least, it was special for me—but now it's over and I have to accept that, no matter how much it hurts.

I'm not surprised by the papers the next day. I'm single, twenty-four and in desperate need of a royal heir or three. And while the news of our betrothal is still confined to an intimate circle of fewer than ten people, Heydar is also young, single and highly eligible. A photograph of us locked in conversation runs in most of the European papers. The headlines are respectful in the more conservative papers, but in the tabloids it's all variation on a theme.

Happily Ever After! A real-life happy ending for the tragic Princess!

And in some, it was more speculative still.

Red-Hot Royal Romance!

Indeed, the photo does make us look quite intimate. Carelessly, I've leaned too close, or perhaps that's him. Our faces are only an inch or so apart, our eyes locked. I try to remember what we were discussing at that moment and draw a blank. The truth is, contrary to the image in front of me, I barely gave Heydar a tenth of my concentration. My entire mind was wrapped up in Santiago and the fact I'd flown out of Spain only hours earlier.

I throw the newspapers aside in a fit of impatience. I have just enough capacity left for rational thought to acknowledge that the photograph can be used to our advantage. When we inevitably announce our marriage, it will seem more realistic. People will believe we are in love.

I grip the wall behind me for support against the horror of that idea.

Another image floods my mind. I see Santiago as he was on the last morning, the way he'd read the newspapers from front to back, and I know there's no way on earth he hasn't seen this. Guilt rips through me and I fight an urge to message him to explain. I owe him nothing, just as he owes me nothing. If he did see the picture, only his ego will care.

I have to let it go.

A week later, at another state dinner, my heart lurches dangerously in my chest and I reach for the Prime Minister's arm, squeezing it unintentionally hard. 'What's *he* doing here?'

Henrik follows my gaze. 'Mr del Almodovár? I invited him, of course.'

'But why?' I turn to face him and am sure I must look as deranged as I feel—overjoyed and terrified all at once. It takes every ounce of will power I possess not to run across the room and throw myself into his arms.

'He's poised to invest billions of dollars into our economy. I thought it made good sense. Speaking of which, have you signed the contract yet, Your Highness?'

I think of the documents I was emailed six days ago, each condition I'd wanted spelled out in clear legalese. Why haven't I signed them? After all, I made up my mind a long time ago. I'm going to sell the land to him. The casino deal will go ahead.

Perhaps Santiago senses my questions, because at that precise moment his head lifts and his eyes pinpoint me effortlessly, slicing through me, exposing me, making me yearn, ache and fly all at once. He murmurs something to the couple he's in conversation with then begins to walk towards me. I have barely any time to brace for his proximity, or to work out how to behave. My instincts are to embrace him, to kiss him, to hold him close and never let go, but this is a very public setting and such a display would be a disaster.

I pull myself up to my full height and straighten my shoulders, aware of both the literal and figurative weight of the diamond tiara I've chosen to wear for the evening. It was my mother's favourite and it seems fitting that I should have that reminder of her tonight, when I am the closest I've ever been to wanting to disregard everything that's expected of me. The spirit of rebellion is almost impossible to tamp down.

Only two feet away from me, Santiago stops, addressing the Prime Minister first, extending a hand and shaking it as if they are old friends.

Seconds later, he turns to me, and I can't work out what's going through his mind. He looks at me and I feel a thousand and one things, but chief amongst them is relief. I thought I'd seen him for the last time, and until this moment I hadn't realised how badly I needed that not to be the case.

The week since I left Spain has been the longest of my life. I have been more isolated and lonely than ever before, more dissatisfied with my gilded cage and the limitations of my role here. Being ceremonially important—and only ceremonially important—is stultifying and infuriating.

I hold my breath, staring at Santiago—I can do nothing more. I'm frozen to the spot.

'Your Highness.' He bows low, the deference so at odds with the way he greeted me in our first meeting that a faint smile crosses my lips.

'Mr del Almodóvar.' My voice shakes a little. 'Thank you for joining us tonight.'

'I was invited,' he says, flicking a glance to the Prime Minister.

'Of course, of course,' Henrik interrupts, so I want to shove him. 'I'm glad you came. Her Highness was just saying she's been meaning to sign the contract.'

'Has she?' Santiago's attention doesn't leave my face.

'I noticed you've incorporated the changes we discussed.' I hope my gratitude shows in my tone.

'I gave you my word that I would.'

My stomach tightens. 'Yes, you did.' I wish Henrik would go away. In fact, I wish everyone would. I want to be alone with Santiago so badly it hurts.

'Well, then, that's settled,' Henrik says convivially, patting Santiago's back. 'Shall we discuss the specifics of your build time?'

Santiago nods once, but his eyes stay on my face. 'However, there are some matters still to clarify with the Princess.'

'Oh?' Hope flutters in my chest. 'There are?'

'Indeed.'

'Shall we do so now?'

'Not tonight.' He gestures to the room. 'It isn't the time, and I'd hate to take you away from your adoring public.' I hear his cynicism, but it's mixed with something else too, an emotion I can't analyse. 'Does tomorrow suit?'

'I can clear my schedule,' I say eagerly—too eagerly, but fortunately Henrik is champing at the bit for this deal to be finalised, presumably so he can announce it ahead of the upcoming election and get the credit for bringing in such a valuable project. If the Prime Minister notices my willingness to meet with Santiago, it only matches his own.

A beat passes. 'You're staying in Marlsdoven tonight?'

A small smile flickers on Santiago's lips. I stare at them, mesmerised. 'If you are free to meet tomorrow, then *sí*.'

'Her Highness has already agreed to it,' Henrik says with over-the-top conviviality. 'Come, let's go and marvel at your site.'

I half-expect—and hope for—Santiago to tell Henrik to get lost. After all, he's not the kind of man to be told what to do or where to go. But he falls into step with the Prime Minister, cutting through the crowd with ease. I watch him go, perturbed and on edge.

Knowing he's here makes it impossible to

concentrate. I rarely drink at events such as this—a message drummed into me when I was first conscious of alcohol and the powers it has to remove barriers—but I murmur a request for a glass of champagne to a palace staff member, grateful when a crisp, cold flute is placed in my hand a moment later.

The first sip is bliss but does little to calm my raging nerves. The evening passes in a blur. I go through the motions—making conversation, smiling, posing for photographs, remembering tidbits about each attendee's life as I have been trained to do—but all the while I'm conscious of Santiago, particularly the way he watches me. I feel his eyes on me and their possessive heat is like a glow building in my chest, burning brighter as the night wears on until finally it's over and I can escape.

All morning I've been waiting for this, yet the moment he strides into the drawing room, my breath catches in my throat and I feel as though my knees will no longer support my weight.

'Mr del Almodóvar,' I murmur, for the benefit of the liveried soldiers who stand sentinel at the doors.

His eyes narrow imperceptibly and the air between us sparks with electricity. He closes the distance slowly, an agonising journey that

makes me want to cry out. I force myself to remember that I'm a princess, and here in Marlsdoven I must behave like it. What we shared in
Spain might as well have taken place between
two different people.

But when his eyes roam my face it is as
though I'm being ravaged. Heat flicks through
me, slowly at first, but then with a flaming urgency burning me so my cheeks are hot and
my lips part.

Finally, he reaches me, his lips twisting in a
cynical half-smile. 'Your Highness.'

His voice runs down my spine like treacle and
I fear my knees might actually buckle if I'm not
careful. I need to sit down but I'm incapable of
moving. I stand there, staring at him for a long
time. The quiet clicking of the door as it closes
rouses me from my stupor.

'Santiago.' Alone now, I use his name, but it's
a form of torture because it reminds me of an
intimacy we can never share again.

'Freja.'

My heart jolts. He's watching me carefully,
his manner apparently relaxed, yet there's a tension on his face that makes me wonder if he's
feeling as many emotions as I am. But of course
he's not. This is Santiago del Almodóvar. What
we shared was earth-shattering and life-chang-
ing for me but for him? It was just another af-

fair in a long string of affairs. I meant nothing. I force myself to remember that as I stare across at him.

'How are you?'

It's a polite question, little more than a civility, but my heart trembles when he asks it.

'Fine,' I lie. There's no sense in telling him that every moment since leaving Spain has been a form of torture…no purpose in telling him that the time we spent together has changed me in a fundamental way. 'And you?'

His response is to lift a shoulder indolently, then gesture to the chairs across the room. 'Shall we get down to business?'

My brows knit together reflexively. 'Oh,' I respond quietly. 'I— Yes. I mean, if you'd like.'

There is a coldness to him that makes me shiver. I feel his distance from me and want to shake him. 'It is why I'm here.'

It's just a statement of fact. It shouldn't bother me but I feel like I'm being pushed into a stream of lava.

'We could have dealt with this over email,' I say with quiet reserve.

'And yet you haven't.' His eyes lance mine. 'You haven't sent the contract back.'

My stomach drops to my toes. He's here for the contract; that's all. No part of this is because he wants to see me. Disappointment is like a chasm in my chest.

'Not for any reason,' I murmur, my voice halting. 'I've just been busy.'

He slices me with a look, as though he knows I'm lying, then moves towards the table set up beneath the window. The contracts have been laid out on it. I watch him from where I stand, watch his autocratic profile as he regards the documents.

'You've read them, I presume?'

I nod, but he's not looking at me.

'Yes.' I walk towards him, my stomach in knots.

'And?' He spins abruptly, pinning me with the full force of his attention so I almost lose my footing.

'Thank you for amending them so completely.' My smile wobbles. 'These terms are more than fair.'

'They're what you requested.'

'I don't think I expected you to grant them.'

'I saw no point in denying you.'

I stand opposite him, hope bursting through me, because surely he's admitting to something more? Surely he was so generous with my requests because he cares for me on some level?

'Why not?' The words rush out of me, husky and desperate.

His eyes narrow. 'Negotiating leads to delays. I want to begin construction immediately.' He looks at the papers once more. 'So, if you're ready?'

Disappointment is fierce. Of course it's business. It's always business with Santiago.

I nod jerkily, but don't reach for the pen.

'I...'

What? What was I going to say?

His eyes pierce mine. He waits. My uncertainty grows. We feel like strangers—no, not strangers. It's worse than that. There's antipathy coming from Santiago, hitting me straight in the face.

'You're angry with me,' I say, sure I'm right.

His only response is to square his jaw.

'Why?' I ask, pushing the point.

'I'm simply impatient for you to sign these documents so our business together is concluded. *Bueno?*'

Frustration slices through me. 'Why are you talking to me like a stranger?'

'Isn't that what we are now?'

My lips part. I go to deny it but pride keeps me silent. I feel the burn of tears behind my eyelids and move quickly, leaning forward and grabbing the pen, staring at the table while I flip through the contract, adding my signature at the bottom of the last page. But when that's done I stay as I am, not wanting him to see the emotion in my eyes, needing a moment to steady myself.

A single tear rolls down my cheek and thuds on the table. Embarrassed, I spin away from him, striding towards the window and staring out at the city without really seeing.

'Thank you.' For a second I think I hear something in his voice, something soft, apologetic even, but then his footsteps sound and I realise he's leaving.

I whirl round, sadness shifting to anger with lightning speed. 'So that's it?' He stops walking but doesn't turn round to face me.

Fury zips across my body. 'Is this how it goes, Santiago? You've had your fun with me and now I'm *persona non grata* to you? I had no idea this is how you treat your ex-lovers.'

At that, he whips round, his eyes like coal.

'How should I treat you, Princesa?'

I flinch at that, the weaponizing of a title he'd made so sexy and intimate now used almost as an insult.

'I'd settle for a modicum of respect—a hint of cordiality.'

A muscle jerks in his jaw. 'Respect?' He strides towards me then, his body emanating tension, his spine ramrod-straight. 'Do you think I am treating you disrespectfully? How, exactly?'

But I can't explain it. It's not anything he's done so much as what he's *not* doing. He's not smiling at me; he's not touching me. He's looking at me as though we're two strangers. He's speaking with icy civility bordering on disdain, but it's only the contrast to how he was in Spain that I resent.

'Forget it,' I say, my voice wobbling with tears. 'Just go.'

'Is that what you want?' he demands quietly.

I stare at him, frustration slicing me. It's not. But what I want isn't possible. I look around me, as if to reinforce that. I'm surrounded by ceremony. This room is one of the oldest parts of the palace. Gold wall panels meet double-height ceilings, crystal chandeliers run in a line down the centre and, at the end of the room, there's a wall of mirrors. The floor is a shining parquetry.

It's a physical reminder of who I am and what I owe my country. Across the corridor is the throne room; he would have walked past it before coming in here. Two golden thrones sit side by side, as they have done for hundreds of years, awaiting occupants.

'Or do you want this?' he asks, purposefully laying the contract back down and rounding the table slowly, giving me time to realise his intention and to stop him if I wish to.

But I don't. Despite the impropriety and impossibility of Santiago I am stationary. Waiting, wanting, needing…

CHAPTER TWELVE

MY BREATH BURNS from my lungs. I stand, waiting, my whole body on alert as he draws me into his arms and kisses me in one motion. His lips press hard against mine, his tongue an invasion, a reminder of his dominance and my surrender. And yet it is also his own surrender. I feel his body's acquiescence to mine, a reminder that there is something bigger than us, something neither can control, overpowering us both.

I groan into his mouth, my arms lifting and wrapping around his neck, my body cleaved to his as I kiss him back harder, hungrier, whimpering with desperation.

He takes a step forward, pinning me against the wall beside the window before lifting me, wrapping my legs around his waist so I feel the force of his arousal against my sex, and I cry out with a visceral, overpowering need.

'Please, Santiago!' I cry, not caring that we're here in this ancient room, not caring for anything right now but coming home again—and, yes, that's exactly what it feels like when we're together. His response is a guttural noise echoed into my throat and then he's pulling me from the wall, surrendering us both to the floor, his hands removing my pants as he pushes up my skirt. My own hands loosen his button and zipper, pushing down his waistband so I can feel his buttocks in the palm of my hand.

Even then, when passion has overtaken me so that I can't think straight, he pauses to provide protection, sheathing himself before driving his length into me so that I cry out, and would have done so longer and louder had he not kissed me, swallowing my noises, muffling my cries with his mouth as his body pleasured mine over and over; driving me to the edge of sanity and then beyond it, before dragging me back to start all over again.

My nails run over the soft fabric of his shirt then dig into his bottom until his own body is racked with pleasure. Finally, his weight collapses on top of me, our breathing rushed, the room a silent witness to something so powerful it shakes me to the core.

I don't know how long we lie there—time seems to have bent beyond recognition—but he stands eventually, turning his back on me as he zips up his trousers. Belatedly, I do the same, shifting and straightening my skirt at the same time. I can't see my panties. It takes me a second to realise he's holding them. My heart lurches.

It was an act of passion but it wasn't like what we shared in Spain. I feel further from him than I did before. I have to understand why.

'Have I done something to offend you?' I ask quietly, moving to him and putting my hand on his chest. His heart thuds, rhythmically but hard.

'No.'

I close my eyes. 'I don't understand. How can you go from making love to me to speaking like this again? I don't get it.'

'There is something I've been wondering,' he says after a beat, his tone cool.

'And that is?'

'Did you kiss him?'

I frown, not understanding what—or who—he's talking about. 'Did you make love with him? Do you feel more for him now than you have previously?' He speaks calmly but there are dark emotions in the depths of his eyes and my pulse fires into overdrive. 'Do you have any idea how I have been tormented by that?'

It's almost conversational, and yet his words stir something deep in my soul. 'That photograph of you and your fiancé was in every newspaper,' he murmurs. 'It was easy to imagine that he'd taken you to bed. And all I could think about was undoing that—coming here and making you mine again, making you beg for me, erasing any memory of him from your mind, erasing his touch from your body.'

He pauses, allowing his words to sink in. 'I did not mean to treat you with disrespect, Freja. I was fighting my own instincts—my base, disgusting instincts to claim you as though you are a possession rather than a woman who can make her own choices. Does that make you happier?'

'Nothing about this makes me happy,' I say quickly, urgently, honestly. 'I didn't sleep with you because of Heydar. I slept with you because I wanted to more than anything in the world.'

His lips form a grim line in his face.

'Are you saying this was just…about ego for you?' I whisper, pressing a hand to my side, digging my nails into my hip.

'I hate the idea of him touching you.' He grips the back of a chair until his knuckles show white. 'I have no right. I know that. But I have been tormented, imagining his hands on your body, your voice calling out his name…'

I shake my head. 'You needn't have worried. I haven't slept with him.'

His skin pales beneath his tan.

'I haven't kissed him,' I add.

His eyes lance mine. 'The photo…'

'Just a glimpse of time. I don't even remember what we were discussing. Nothing important.'

He nods slowly, but if I'd expected relief on his features there is none.

'You still intend to marry him?'

My heart rips apart. God, how I wish things were different. I look around the room, trying to draw strength from my surroundings, but all I feel is weakened by them—weakened, vulnerable and resentful. 'Yes.'

He looks away from me, and for a second I feel as though he's fighting some kind of battle, but when he speaks it's with his trademark confidence. 'When?'

'Three months after my coronation.'

He pins me with his eyes. 'Be mine, until then.'

A shiver runs down my spine. 'What does that mean?'

'It means I want you. Until you're married, I want you to be mine.'

Nothing makes sense. I stare at him, trying to think this through, part of me elated and part of me devastated. I can't explain why I feel either emotion, just that both are overtaking me.

'It just doesn't… I don't see how…' I shake my head with frustration, trying to clarify my thoughts. 'Spain only worked because it was a secret. Here, in Marlsdoven, I'm surrounded. I can't pick up where we left off. If someone found out and it got into the press…particularly once my engagement's announced…'

His body is stiff. 'No one will find out.'

'How can you be so sure.'

He pulls a key out of his pocket, handing it to me. 'I have an apartment in the city. You can go there any time. There's an undercover parking garage. No one will ever see you.'

'And then what?' I ask, numb.

'What do you mean?'

'One day I get married and we simply stop seeing each other?'

Determination fires his voice. 'I won't sleep with another man's wife.'

My eyes sweep shut at his ability to speak with such clinical detachment. It's a skill I seem to lack where this man's concerned.

'What you're offering is very tempting.'

He stares, waiting for me to continue. I turn away, finding it impossible to think with him watching me so intently.

'But I can't do it.'

It's as though I've been struck by lightning. I understand why his offer is hurting me so much, why it's leaving me with the sense I have a hole in my heart.

'Because someone might see us together?' he responds with a dark emotion I can't interpret.

'No. Yes. Partly.' I furrow my brow. 'That would obviously be…less than ideal, and there's a risk of it happening, despite the fact your apartment has a secure garage.'

I can feel his condemnation even without turning to face him.

'I know you can't possibly understand, but the scandal would be disastrous. Particularly if it's after my engagement has been announced.'

I hear a puff of air, a sound of derision.

'Like I said, what you're suggesting is very tempting, and if I were free to do whatever I wanted then I'd probably agree. But I'm not free, Santiago. I'm not free and never will be.'

'You are martyring yourself,' he accuses coldly.

'Martyring myself? No. I'm serving my people and their needs above my own, as I always have and always will.'

'Serve them, by all means, but it's the twenty-first century. Find a way to live your own life too.'

'And what does that entail?' I demand, turning the tables on him. 'What are you suggesting? What life should I lead? Have an affair with you until you tire of me and move on—exposing me to ridicule and public sympathy as a jilted ex-lover of the great Santiago del Almodóvar? Can you imagine what my parents would say?'

His eyes narrow, his face taut.

'And we both know you *will* tire of me. Because this is all you're offering, right?' I gesture towards the floor we just made love on. 'Memorable but meaningless sex—secret, shameful assignations and no future?'

'You are the one who's ashamed,' he responds quickly, then changes course. 'Do you want a future with me?'

My lips part, my brow clammy. I shake my head once, even when my heart is bursting with desperation to say, *yes, that's exactly what I want!*

'So what is the problem, then?' he demands, eyes narrowing.

I stare across at him, an ache in my chest widening into the worst pain I've ever felt.

'You have said many times that you cannot be seen with me, that no one can know about this. I get it. As ridiculous as I think that is, my ego is secure enough to not care. But if you cannot be seen with me, you sure as hell cannot marry me, so don't act as though you're holding out for a proposal.'

'I'm not,' I whisper, even as I think maybe I am. I realise it sounds ludicrous. We've known each other such a short amount of time, but none of that matters, because I *know* him. On every level I know him, and I love him, and I want to spend my life with him. It's an impossible fantasy.

'But what if I wasn't going to marry Heydar?' I push with soft determination. 'What if I was free to do what I wanted with my life? You still wouldn't be proposing to me.'

He drags a hand through his hair, pinning me with the intensity of his gaze. 'I have never wanted to marry anyone.'

I bite down on my lower lip to stop myself from reacting.

'And you have to have children. There is no hypothetical to negate the importance of that. Right?'

'Right.' I clear my throat, the chasm between us widening to an insurmountable distance. 'Which brings me back to the stupidity of continuing this. It's just going to lead to one or both of us getting really badly hurt, okay?'

'Hurt how?'

My heart breaks at that. It shows how little he cares for me that he can't even grasp what I'm getting at.

'You sleep with a lot of women. I get it. Sex is just sex for you. It means nothing.'

His brow creases.

'But I'm…not like that. You'll always be my first and, despite the fact that I know how transient this is, I care about you.'

He nods slowly, as though only just starting to comprehend. 'And you're worried you might fall in love with me?'

I close my eyes, the truth thick in my throat.

'You won't, Freja. You're too smart for that.'

I make a scoffing noise. 'Believe me, it's risky. I have to marry Heydar, and I can't do that if I'm pining for you. I need a clean break, time to get over you and move on with my life. We had fun in Spain but it needs to stay there.'

He speaks as though I haven't spoken. 'You're worried about falling in love with me, but I don't see any risk there. Not when we're both so honest about what this is and what we want.'

His calm argument is the breaking of all my resolve. 'That's just the thing, Santiago. I'm not being honest with you.'

He frowns. I suck in a breath, steeling myself to be brave. 'I'm already in love with you, and if I keep seeing you, sleeping with you, I'm terrified I won't be strong enough to walk away from you. I'm terrified that I'll love you so much I'll turn my back on everything I have to do—and I can't let that happen, okay? So just…stop arguing and let it go.'

He stares at me for several seconds, surprise

on his face. Whatever hope I'd cherished that he might turn round and say he loves me too dies with every second that passes.

'Freja…' My name is a groan on his lips. Sadness engulfs me.

'You're asking me to give up everything that matters to me because your ego's been hurt by the fact I'm betrothed to another guy. I can't turn my back on my people and palace because you're not ready to let me go yet, because you like having sex with me.'

He shakes his head as if to dismiss this. 'It's more than that. It's a connection. There's chemistry between us, and it's breath-taking and urgent. That's why I don't want to let you go.' My lips part; dreaded hope returns. 'But that's not love. It's just great sex. If you had more experience, you'd understand that.'

I flinch, rejecting that with every fibre of my DNA. My voice is roughened by emotion. 'And maybe if you had a little less experience you'd be less jaded and see what's standing right in front of you. This is more than just great chemistry.'

He expels a heavy sigh. 'If you feel that way, then why fight this? Why not enjoy what we share for a few more months? This is not complicated, Freja.'

The fact he thinks so is further evidence—

as though I need any—of how little he cares for me.

'If I keep sleeping with you it will kill me. Already the idea of never seeing you again is like acid in my gut. The thought of marrying someone else and having them touch me, kiss me, make love to me, is anathema. Don't you get that?'

'You think I like the idea? Hell, that photo of the two of you together made me want to kill him, and I am not a violent person, Freja.'

A burst of heat runs the length of my spine. 'Doesn't that tell you something?'

'It tells me that I feel possessive of you, that I don't like sharing. But none of these things is love.' He drops his head, his forehead pressing to mine.

'And that's why we have to walk away.' And I do just that, taking a step back, staring at him from eyes that are smarting with unshed tears.

'Eventually, but not now.'

'It has to be now.' I press my hand to his chest, feeling the beating of his heart, wishing it were beating for me. 'I won't be strong enough later, and you're not offering me enough. This isn't enough…'

'What do you want, then?' he demands, his voice rising.

'I want all of you!' I roar back, forgetting

where I am for a moment. I grind my teeth together. 'I want you to love me back. I want you to want me in your bed, not just for the next few months, but for the rest of our lives. I want you to beg me not to marry Heydar. I want you to want me like I want you.'

His eyes flare wide, his cheeks slashed with dark colour. 'That's not possible.'

'Why not?'

He makes a harsh laughing sound. 'You're the one who told me how unsuitable I am for you, how your people would react if they got wind of our affair. Have you changed your mind?'

I gape at him because he's right, and I'd forgotten momentarily. 'I'm not saying it's straightforward, but if you loved me maybe we could find a way…'

His eyes glint when they meet mine. I am on tenterhooks.

'If you loved me,' I whisper, 'Anything would be possible.'

He takes a step back, and I am reminded of all the times he pushed me away when we were in Barcelona. I gasp, because I know what's coming even before he speaks.

'I'm offering a casual relationship. An extension of what we shared in Spain, nothing more. I have no intention of asking you to do anything that would permanently change the course of your life. You've decided to marry him. It's important to you, and I accept that.'

'And that's it?' I ask quietly. 'You really don't care?'

He lifts his shoulders in a casual shrug, but every molecule of him reverberates with tension. 'I disagree with the premise of an arranged marriage…'

I wave my hand through the air. 'And that's it?' I repeat angrily.

'What more do you want me to say? Do you want me to tell you I don't love you? That I don't love anyone? That hearing you say you love me is the absolute last thing I want?'

I spin away from him, my heart in a thousand pieces. *I don't love you.*

'All this time, you've accused me of living my life for other people, but at least there's a purpose to my choices. You push everyone away because you're terrified of getting close to another soul.'

'I am not afraid.'

'Liar,' I mutter. 'You stand there and tell me you don't love me, but I don't think you even know how you feel. You're clinging to a self-protective mechanism you developed decades ago, even when it's destroying your life.'

'I'm perfectly happy in my life.'

'How can you be when you're so alone?'

'Alone is the last thing I am.'

I suck in a deep breath, his words like a sledgehammer at my side.

I spin round to face him in time to see him pick up the contract. 'You're right, Your Highness. There's no future here. You want more than I could ever give you—or anyone.'

'It's a beautiful day, Your Highness.'

I blink across at Claudia, a frown on my face. 'Sorry?'

She gestures to the window I'm sitting at, pointing at the blue sky. 'Why don't we go for a drive into the country? Have a picnic somewhere, hmm?'

My smile is tight and dismissive. 'I appreciate what you're trying to do, but it's not necessary. I'm fine.'

We haven't discussed the details of my love life. Three weeks ago, I came back to my apartment with tear-streaked cheeks and Claudia drew me into her arms and held me. Without knowing what happened—though I'm sure she's guessed some of it—she knew I was devastated. Since then, she's been a godsend, clearing my schedule as much as possible, minimising any requirements for me to go out in the world, to be seen and behave as normal.

I don't feel normal.

I feel broken in a way that must be obvious to anyone who looks at me.

'At some point, you're going to have to face this,' she says gently, propping her hips on the desk at my side, studying my face with worry.

'Face what?'

Her sigh is just audible. 'Whatever is making you feel like this. Why don't you tell me about it?'

My eyes clamp shut. I remember how certain Claudia was that Santiago was every bit as bad as his reputation, but the truth is she was wrong. He's nothing like people assume, but for me that's even worse. Loving him was too easy.

'I can't.' My voice cracks.

She sighs again. 'Then tell me what I can do to help.'

I'm tempted to respond with 'nothing', but suddenly it occurs to me that that's not true. My eyes widen as realisation starts to firm inside my chest. I rejected Santiago because of duty––a duty to my parents and my people, a wish to do them proud. Becoming another notch on Santiago's bedpost would have been insupportable. I walked away from the only man I've ever loved because it was the right thing to do. And now I have to take the next step, cementing the break between us, making it impossible for me to change my mind. He was offering sex, that's all. How could he have expected me to jeopardise my reputation for something he sees as meaningless?

I fix Claudia with a cool stare, but as I speak I feel as though my heart is turning to ice. 'Would you contact Heydar for me? I'd like to meet with him for lunch.'

CHAPTER THIRTEEN

'THANK YOU FOR meeting me,' I say quietly, nerves fluttering inside my belly.

'Of course. It would be poor form to turn down a lunch invitation from the woman I'm to marry.'

I move quickly, so the fork to my left clatters to the ground. I wince apologetically and dip down to retrieve it. Per my request, he and I are alone on the balcony, just the two of us—no staff to overhear this very private conversation and, more importantly, no chance of a photographer capturing this moment.

'That's what I wished to speak to you about.'

'The wedding?' He nods. 'I suppose it's time. Your coronation is set for three months?'

I toy with the stem of my wine glass. 'Yes.'

'And three months later, we'll tie the knot?'

A lump forms in my throat. 'I didn't know about our engagement until after they'd died.' I fix my gaze on the view beyond him. The city sprawls beneath us, elegant and ancient.

He shifts his head to the side. 'My parents told me when I was a teenager. I had been dating a girl, and they felt it fair to prepare me for my future.'

I bite down on my lower lip. 'I wish my parents had told me in person, but I suppose they thought there wasn't a need. I would have liked a chance to discuss this with them.'

'Understandably.'

He's so *nice*, so patient. I wish more than anything that I cared for him, but I don't. At least, not enough. 'After they died, I became fixated on doing absolutely everything I could just as they would have wished. I imagined them beside me often——heard their praise, feared their disappointment and drew comfort from any opportunity that showed me clearly how they'd wish me to behave.'

My eyes bore into his. 'Marrying you is something I've never questioned, because I know how happy it would have made them. I think that in marrying you it would be a like bringing them back, in some way.' I shake my head. 'It's very hard to explain.'

'I understand,' he agrees gently.

And I really think he does. 'I want them to

be proud of me, but lately I've come to realise that I can't ignore my own instincts completely.'

He sips his water, waiting for me to continue.

'Marrying you because our parents wished it doesn't make sense. Not any more.' Santiago's eyes fill my mind, giving me courage, even when I know the future I'm carving out for myself doesn't involve him.

'I've always wanted to live my life following the blueprint my parents laid out for me, but I've come to understand that doesn't entail doing everything just as they might have wished. It's about living with decency and honour, about loving this kingdom and country so much that I always work to make it better and safer, more prosperous, for our people. A blueprint isn't necessarily about ticking items off a list, but being true to a set of core values, values they drove into me since birth. But it's also about balance.'

I fold my hands in my lap. 'I'm not just a princess. I'm a person too. And while my country deserves my best it doesn't deserve all of me. I can't marry a man I don't love, Heydar. No matter how much my parents wished it. I'm sorry.'

His eyes probe mine and I hold my breath, worried he'll be angry, worried he'll try to convince me. But after a moment he smiles. 'Perhaps you'll fall in love with me over time?'

But he's joking, or at least not serious.

'I won't,' I respond firmly. 'I wish I could,' I add after a moment. 'But, as it turns out, it's not possible.'

'No?'

I shake my head, refusing to be drawn on the matter of Santiago, yet I suspect he understands what I'm not saying.

'In trying to live my life as my parents would have wished, I think I've been ignoring one of their most important lessons—to be true to myself. I can't go through with it. I'm sorry.'

'Don't apologise.' He stands and moves to the railing, looking down over the view I love so much. 'I'm surprised, of course. I fully intended our wedding to go ahead. But I respect your decision.' He turns to face me. 'I adored your parents, you know.'

My heart skips a beat.

'Your father was a frequent visitor at our palace. He was a funny, kind man.'

My smile is immediate. 'Yes, he was.'

'And I believe you're right. He would wish you to follow your heart, Freja, and it clearly isn't leading you to me.'

I shake my head silently.

'May I make one suggestion, though?'

'Yes, of course.'

'What if we become friends? I think that would have made our parents happiest of all.'

Relief bursts through me. 'I'd like that, Heydar. I really would.'

'Have you had a chance to peruse the plans yet, Your Highness?'

I blink at Henrik before shaking my head. 'I'm sorry. Plans for what?'

'The del Almodovár construction.'

'Oh.' Heat lashes me. It's been three months since I last saw Santiago and I can barely hear his name without breaking out in a sweat. I miss him in a way that defies reason and sense. I dream of him every night without fail. Well, not dream, exactly, because to dream I would have to sleep, and I find that sleep mostly eludes me. But I remember him. I impose him into my life and my bed, so that I reach for him at all hours and imagine his hands on my body. It is frustrating and soul-destroying, so each morning I wake with a deeper sense of loneliness than the day before.

I have deliberately avoided doing anything to make this harder, which includes typing his name into an Internet search browser or looking at the information I'm being bombarded with about the casino.

'You should see how the design has panned

out,' my Prime Minister continues. 'I think you'll like the direction he's taken the project in.'

'I will,' I lie. 'I just haven't had a moment.'

'Of course. Your coronation preparations must be in full swing.'

I force a smile to my face.

'You will come to the ground-breaking, though?' he asks. 'The media will be there. It's important, I think, that you are seen to support the project.'

My eyes close for a moment and then I nod. I know I can't ignore it. Henrik is right. My absence would indeed be conspicuous. 'Yes, I'll be at the ground-breaking, Henrik.'

The moment my car pulls up I see him. How can I not? Even in a crowd of faces, Santiago is impossible to miss—tall, broad-shouldered, wearing jeans, and a dark jacket in deference to the fact the temperature has turned cool. I dig my fingernails into my palms to stop myself from doing something truly stupid, such as running to him.

I want to.

I want to so badly.

But I can't.

For one thing, everything's changed between us. He hasn't called or texted since that morning in the palace three and a half months ago. I don't doubt that he's moved on, though thank God I have no confirmation of that. To see photographs of him with another woman would kill me.

The door to my car is opened and the crowd grows quiet. In the distance, there are rope garlands with people lined up behind them. I must greet them first, before I join the assembly of officials. I step out of the car and an enormous cheer erupts. Without needing to look in his direction, I feel his eyes on me, their intensity searing my soul.

Walking towards the first cluster of people, I accept a bouquet of flowers and a teddy bear. I stop and chat to an old woman, who remembers meeting my mother, then a young girl, who is dressed in a gown and tiara. She gives me a hand-written invitation to her birthday party, and as I hand it to Claudia I whisper to ask her to send cupcakes as a birthday present. On and on it goes, for twenty minutes at least, before finally I'm at the end of the line and Henrik awaits.

'Your Highness…' The Prime Minister beams from ear to ear. 'How delightful to see you.'

I focus on his face, but it doesn't matter. My peripheral vision has picked up Santiago. I'm aware of his proximity and know that I must soon come face to face with him. I don't know if I have the strength for this.

Claudia, beside me, puts her hand briefly on mine, squeezing it, and I know then that she understands. She's pieced it all together. Her gesture does indeed give me some strength.

Turning to face Santiago is like being struck by lightning.

He is the same, but different. His hair has been cut shorter, and I see that what I had thought were jeans are actually the dark trousers of the suit he wears. There is no tie, but he looks so formal compared to usual garb. His dark eyes stare through me, and my heart rabbits against my ribs so hard it hurts.

'Your Highness.' He bows low. 'Thank you for coming.'

It's a perfectly respectable greeting that gives little away. I force myself to smile, but it's almost impossible. 'Naturally.'

'There's a shovel over here!' Henrik's tone is jolly, perfectly at odds with the depth of my feelings.

'I understand you are going to dig the car park?' Santiago murmurs in a light joke.

I don't smile. 'Just a ceremonial shovel, I'm afraid. No free labour today.'

'Pity. Car parks are always the most expensive part.'

I lift my eyes to him and feel as though the world has tipped completely off its axis. I lose my footing a little but he shoots a hand out to steady me, pressing it to my elbow then releasing again just as quickly—almost as if I imagined it, as if he can't bear to touch me.

I stare at him, stricken, panic making it impossible to think straight. People are watching. Photographers are everywhere.

'Your Highness?' Claudia's voice drags me back to reality. 'This way, please.' She inserts herself between Santiago and me, gesturing towards a small timber platform that's been erected for the purpose of today.

I've done this sort of thing dozens of times in my life, yet my hands shake when I'm given the shovel.

Henrik makes a short speech about the importance of design innovation and the twenty-first century, the impressive work Del Almodóvar Industries has achieved around the world and the promise for a new generation that this precinct will bring.

There is applause when he's finished, and then I do my part—smiling brightly as I wield the shovel, delicately sifting dirt around to ensure the press pool has a chance to get a decent photograph of the historic moment.

I hate to think what my father would say.

* * *

'Princesa, wait.'

His voice is low, something in the tone causing my feet to slow. I'm within sight of my car. Another minute and I'll escape.

'Freja.' He speaks my name low enough that only Claudia and I hear.

I stop walking and turn to face him, not even capable of offering a civil smile.

Up close, and almost alone with him, my legs feel completely hollowed out.

'Mr del Almodóvar,' I murmur. 'What can I do for you?'

He's frustrated and annoyed by that. His eyes flash to mine, irritation obvious in their depths. 'I'd like a moment of your time.'

Panic flares in my breast. I cannot tell you how badly I want that too. I shake my head. 'It's not possible. I'm sorry.'

'Then when will it be possible?' he demands, his teeth bared.

'Her Highness's schedule is quite full,' Claudia offers.

'I believe Her Highness can speak for herself,' Santiago responds with icy disdain.

I glare at him, then turn to Claudia. 'It's fine.' I put a reassuring hand on her arm. 'I'll meet you in the car.'

Alone with him, I speak quietly. 'There are

people and cameras everywhere. Please remember that.'

'Have you looked at the plans?'

This is what he wishes to discuss—the bloody plans?

I shake my head. 'I sold the land to you, Mr del Almodóvar. The nature of your casino construction is no longer of interest to me.'

He swears in Spanish, low in his throat. 'Stop calling me that, as though I mean nothing to you, or I'll kiss you right here to prove what a liar you are.'

I gasp, my eyes flaring wide.

'You wouldn't dare!'

'Try me.' He stares at me for several seconds then shakes his head with obvious frustration. 'I don't care what your plans are this afternoon. Cancel them and come to my apartment.'

I know for a fact my schedule is empty, courtesy of a vigilant Claudia, but I don't tell him that. 'Why?'

'To discuss the plans, for a start. Do you still have a key?'

I shake my head. 'I threw it away.'

I can see that angers him. I'm strangely pleased.

'Fine. Call me when you get there and I'll buzz you in.'

'It's not—'

'Seriously, Freja. Do not fight me on this. I'm not above dragging you into my car.'

CHAPTER FOURTEEN

'WHAT IS IT?'

My pulse is rushing so loudly in my ears, it's all I can hear. Alone with Santiago in his apartment, I feel the ghosts of past heartbreak and they're threatening to eat me alive.

'Please, come in.'

He gestures into the penthouse. It's nothing like I'd expected. Elegant and somehow homely. Not the blank-slate hotel décor I was imagining.

I grind my teeth together, hating that we are like strangers now, hating the distance between us, hating that I'm pretending to be angry at him when I'm actually just angry at the impossibility of our situation.

'No security guards?'

'I thought it best to keep this visit completely off the record,' I murmur.

'Heaven forbid anyone should know you came here.'

My heart stammers. 'What did you want to discuss?'

He drags a hand through his hair, pinning me with his gaze. 'Many things.'

My stomach swoops. 'I don't have long.'

His jaw clenches. 'Have a seat, Princesa.'

I startle, opening my mouth to snap back something at him, but then I close it again. Fighting with him only ever leads to one thing. I move to the table and pull back a chair, settling into it with a straight spine.

He brings me a cup of coffee without actually offering one. I nod my thanks. Then he's quiet, striding the length of the table before stopping, staring at me for a second and turning on his heel, striding back. I watch, flummoxed and confused, my heart in my throat.

'Here.' He grabs something off the table and brings it to me. I recognise the papers—his logo is emblazoned on the corners.

I ignore it. 'I told you. I'm not interested in seeing your casino plans.'

He makes a noise that is a cross between a laugh and a furious grunt. 'Damn it, stop being so stubborn and look.' He opens the book in front of me, and for a few seconds I continue to stare resolutely ahead before concluding it's childish to the extreme.

'Fine,' I huff, focussing on the illustrations.

I expected them to be a version of what had first passed my desk over a year ago, but these are completely different. Frowning, I look more closely.

MARLSDOVEN CROWN ARTS PRECINCT

I lift a hand to my mouth, clamping it there, tears filling my eyes. It doesn't make any sense. My fingertips tremble as I turn the page and study the drawings in more detail. Enormous glass structures to capture the river views and exquisite park-land are punctuated by tall, modern towers that spear into the sky, each housing accommodation. Two are marked as residential, one as offices and an additional two as hotels.

The glass constructions are labelled neatly: library, performance arena, art gallery. There are several wrap-around balconies and restaurants.

My fingers trace the drawings and I shake my head. 'It's like you've reached into my mind and created a fantasy.'

'That was, more or less, the brief.'

I jerk my face to his, not understanding. 'But Santiago, why? This isn't… You're building a casino.'

His eyes burn into me with an intensity that takes my breath away. 'I no longer have any interest in casinos.'

'What do you mean?'

'I sold that part of my business.'

My jaw drops. I lift a hand to his shoulder. Despite the fact I'm sitting down, I feel like I need support, or a reminder of reality. Nothing makes sense. 'I'm sorry. I'm struggling to understand. How can that be?'

'The casinos are incredibly lucrative. It was not difficult to find a buyer.'

'But you're—they're a part of what you do. You love them.'

'I did,' he agrees with a nod. 'But not any more.'

'When did you decide this? Why didn't you tell me last time we met?'

'I hadn't arranged it then.' He stands up, moving away from me. I stare at the chair he had just occupied, my mind sluggish in the face of these revelations.

'I understand from your Prime Minister that the date of your coronation has been brought forward to April?'

'Yes,' I confirm numbly.

'I see.'

Silence falls between us, sharp and uncomfortable. I am conscious of his breathing, heavier than usual. I sense that he wishes to say something else, but he doesn't.

I fill the silence eventually. 'Your apartment's nice. Do you live here?'

He turns to face me, but he seems distracted. '*Si.*'

My breath catches in my throat; it takes all my willpower to seem perfectly calm in the face of that admission. 'Since when?'

'Since a week after…we last saw one another.'

'Oh.' I stumble over the word, my mind spinning. All this time, he was within miles of my palace? When I was looking out over this city, craving him, missing him, he was right here?

'I don't understand why you did this.' I run a finger over the plans. 'But I'm…grateful, I think.'

'You think?'

'I don't know. I feel…guilty, too. That casino was your dream.'

'Not any more.'

I frown, standing and moving to his side. 'Santiago, what happened?'

'If I built that casino, you would have come to hate me.' He spears me with his eyes. 'And, every day you looked out on it, you would have hated me more. I realised I couldn't live with that.'

'I wouldn't hate you for that.'

'Of course you would. And you should. One day, someone will build a casino in Marlsdoven,

Freja. I believe it's inevitable. But that person will not be me.'

I had come to terms with his damned casino; I had loved him despite it. And yet now gratitude steamrollers into love, and I feel as though I'm going to turn into a blubbering mess. I've already thrown myself at Santiago once, though, and made a fool of myself by declaring my unwanted love. For months I have lived with the pain of his rejection. I won't do it again. I have to get out of here before I say too much.

'Thank you.' I scrape the chair back abruptly, standing and moving around the table, putting furniture between us out of desperation. He watches me with a haunted look in his eyes.

'Why did you bring the coronation forward?'

My own response is quiet. 'Why not?' I run my finger over the chair-back. 'My destiny has been plotted out for me since birth. Why delay the inevitable?'

A muscle jerks in the base of his jaw. 'I see.'

I swallow past a lump in my throat. *Leave, now.* 'Well…' I pull on the strap of my handbag, trying to smile. 'If that's everything…?' What kind of fool am I that even now I hope he'll say something, that he'll offer me what I desperately want?

But he's quiet. Watchful. His body is tense, shoulders held firm.

And, as I turn to leave, he doesn't try to stop me. Every footstep draws me further from him until my hand is on the door, turning the handle.

'Wait.' His voice is no longer commanding. It's heavy with surrender, desperate. 'Stop a moment.'

My shoulders slump because, for all that I'd been hoping he would stop me, I can't take much more of this.

'I have to go. Claudia's waiting in the car.'

He swears under his breath, so I turn to look at him. He runs a hand over the back of his neck, staring at the plans on the table. My heart twists.

'So everything is confirmed?'

I frown. 'I don't understand. With the building?'

'No, Princesa.' His features are haunted. 'With your marriage.'

All the air rushes out of me. 'I...' It hadn't even occurred to me that he wouldn't know. But why should he? My engagement to Heydar hadn't been public knowledge, and there's been no report in the press that we've broken it.

'Just tell me.' Now it's Santiago's turn to grip the back of the chair as though he needs the support. 'I appreciate that you're trying to choose the right words, but I would prefer to have the facts.'

My lips part in confusion. He sounds so wounded, as though his whole life rides on the status of my betrothal. Why?

'Will it happen soon?'

I shake my head, anguished.

'When?'

'We're not getting married.'

His head whips up to face mine. For a second, it's as though he can't speak. He stares at me, reading me, as if perhaps I'm lying—though for what purpose, I can't say.

'You're not getting married?'

'Not to Heydar,' I respond with a small shrug. 'But one day, I guess.'

'What happened?' The words rush out of him, startling me.

'Does it matter?'

'Humour me.'

I shake my head.

'Please.'

With a sigh, I pull on my handbag strap once more. 'Are you looking for more ego stroking, Santiago? Do you want to hear that it's because of you?'

'Was it?'

'Well, partly. It didn't seem very fair to marry Heydar when I was in love with someone else.'

He drags a hand through his hair so it stands

up at odd angles. 'And are you still in love with me, Princesa?'

I blink at the question, my heart in my throat. I can't deny how I feel, but at the same time I'm furious with him for asking me.

'Forget I asked. I have no right. I'm sorry.'

I don't understand what's happening. I spin back to the door, but now I hear him moving, his footsteps quick. Just as I open the door, his arm reaches past me, pushing it closed again. I spin round, angry, but the look of resignation on his features silences me. His head is bent, and I know enough about agony to recognise it in someone else.

'Let me tell you something before you leave. Please.'

That word again! It's so unlike Santiago. I nod crisply but don't remove my hand from the door.

'The day at the palace...'

I groan, because I don't want to go back there. I don't want to think about the way we argued, about the way he told me he didn't love me.

'I was so angry. That photograph of the two of you was all I could think of, Freja. It tormented me and came to life inside me, so by the time I saw you I was filled with darkness. I came to Marlsdoven hoping to prove that what I felt for you was all in my head.'

I look away. 'I see.'

'No, you don't. Because, even if that was my intention, I hadn't been at the palace for more than two minutes before I realised how complicated this is. How much I'd missed you. I couldn't take my eyes off you. You were so beautiful, so regal, so incredibly confident. And I was proud of you—proud that even for a few nights I was a man you wanted to be with. But it was all an illusion—you'd never really be mine. There was always Heydar and that photo in the back of my mind.'

'It was just a picture.'

'I found it impossible to believe that.'

I breathe out slowly, dropping my hand from the doorknob.

'I don't know if this post mortem is helpful,' I say honestly. 'That morning was one of the worst of my life. I'll never forget how it felt to tell you that I loved you and have you—'

'Please don't.' He lifts a finger to my lips. 'Don't remember that morning. Not like that.'

'How should I remember it?'

'I knew you were different to anyone I'd ever been with, but since the first moment we met I've been fighting you—telling myself one more night would be enough, then another and another. And until that morning I'd never understood why I refused to see what was right in front of me.'

'But you do now?'

His smile is ghostly. 'Only because you made me understand. No one has ever loved me before. Not my parents, no one. You told me you loved me, and gave me something I wanted so much, but what if you took it away again? What if I let myself love you and you decided you were wrong? What if you married him anyway, and I could never love you? What if I had to live the rest of my life knowing you were out of my reach? I tried to convince us both that this is just sex, because sex is safe and I understand it. But it was never that with us, Freja. It was never just that.'

My knees are tingling.

'I didn't change the plans because I had any hope of winning you back. But I love you, and that means I want to make you happy—with all that I am, for the rest of my life. Even if all hope is lost.'

I shuffle backwards, pressing my spine to the door. 'You love me,' I repeat, nodding slowly, as if to commit his words to memory.

'Of course.'

There! A glimmer of his trademark arrogance shines through. I slant him a sidelong glance, but the cynicism I'm going for is ruined by the sheen of tears in my eyes. After four months of heartbreak, I don't know if I can believe him so easily.

'Why haven't you called?'

'And say what? I thought you were getting married to him? Worse, I thought you'd brought the wedding plans forward? And what could I say? That I realised too late I'm completely in love with you? You deserve better than that. All I could hope was that you were happy, even if that was without me.'

'You're telling me this now?' I point out, my pulse ravaging my system.

'You're not engaged any more.'

I mull on that.

'I didn't deserve you then, Freja. I don't deserve you now. But at least by giving you this…' he gestures to the windows and the view of what will become his construction site '… I'm honouring you in a way that will bring you joy—the kind of joy, I hope, that those few days in Spain gave me.' He lifts his hands to cup my cheeks, staring into my eyes. 'Those days were the best of my life.'

It's too much. I lift a hand to his chest, curling my hands in his shirt for a second, tempted to drag him close—except instead I push him away. He's surprised and moves backward without much effort.

'Damn you, Santiago. Why didn't you realise this four months ago?'

He nods unevenly. 'I know. It's too late.'

'It's not that.' Again, I lift my hand to his chest, not pushing him away now. 'It's just—do you have any idea what I've been through? To love someone like I love you and think they don't feel the same way?'

'You were so brave,' he says quietly. 'To admit how you felt, even with all the obstacles we faced. You do realise nothing's changed, Freja? I'm still someone your people will be scandalised by.' He leans forward, his eyes probing mine. 'I want to be in your life, but we have to work out how to do that to avoid a scandal. I believe this apartment gives us an opportunity to see one another without anyone ever finding out.'

'No.'

His face tightens. He's afraid I'm rejecting him. And for a second I'm in awe of the power I apparently wield over this man. But I can't let him feel pain for a moment longer. 'That's not good enough. I don't want you to be some illicit secret. I'm not ashamed of you. I truly believe you are the best man in the world, and if anyone has a problem with our relationship then it's exactly that: their problem.'

His eyes widen, but he shakes his head. 'I

can't let you do that. I know what your role means to you.'

All my pleasure evaporates as I realise the glaring flaw in our plan. He loves me, but he's not offering me the things I need. For a moment I'd forgotten, but I can't just have a secret boyfriend in an apartment near the city. 'For how long?' I ask quietly.

'What do you mean?'

'How long will you stay? For as long as the construction is going on?'

His brow furrows.

'Because I do need to get married one day, and have children. I know how you feel about those things, but I can't ignore all my obligations…'

'You misunderstand me—but that's my fault, not yours.' Before I realise what he's doing, Santiago del Almodóvar bends down on one knee, his hand on my hip. 'The greatest privilege in my life would be marrying you and raising our children with you. I know it's an uphill journey, that my reputation will take some work to overcome, but there is nothing I have ever wanted more. And when I want something, *querida,* I move mountains to get it.'

I laugh, a laughter born of sheer, overpowering happiness. 'I know that.'

'Wait.'

He stands quickly and walks into the kitchen, opening a drawer before returning and kneeling down once more. He holds up a small velvet box.

Despite what he's just said, this feels so much more real now. I find it hard to breathe. He lifts the lid and the most beautiful ring I've ever seen stares back at me. An enormous bright white diamond stands in the centre, surrounded by a circlet of black diamonds. 'It reminded me of you,' he says after a moment. 'It made me think about goodness overpowering darkness. It's how I've felt every day since knowing you.'

I kneel down then, ignoring the ring, despite its beauty. 'I need you to know something,' I say quietly.

'Go on.' I hear his fear, and a small sob tears through me despite my happiness.

'Please don't look like that. I will never stop loving you. There is nothing you can do, nothing you can say, that will change how I feel. I love you for who you are in here.' I press a hand to his heart. 'Because you are good and kind and thoughtful and, when I'm with you, I feel as though there's nothing in the world I can't do.' I soften my voice. 'But I will always regret implying that your reputation is something to be ashamed of. Everything you've done in life, all your choices, have made you who you are, and I am lucky beyond words that you love me as I do you. Do you understand?'

In the end, any worry about Santiago being accepted by my country was completely unnecessary. His billion-euro investment certainly paved the way—barely any mention of his existence before me was made. And, thanks to a few well-placed interviews, the narrative of Santiago's life had a far more accurate bearing on the truth of his character than the tabloid junk I'd seen in the past.

His reputation as a courageous fighter who overcame adversity to make his mark in the world was written about in all the papers, so too was his philanthropic endeavours. Even I didn't realise how much of his fortune he donates to child poverty and anti-hunger initiatives each year. By the time our wedding day rolls around, I know two things for sure: there is no one on earth who will make a better Queen's Consort and the people of Marlsdoven love Santiago almost more than they do me.

I have no nerves. No anxiety. Only excitement. The chapel is packed with family and friends—Heydar and his brothers sit in the front row, on my side. Santiago's parents are absent, and I didn't force the issue. It doesn't matter; the love surrounding us is palpable. Claudia serves as my Maid of Honour and is genuinely over-joyed for me. The train of my dress is almost half as long as the chapel's aisle, far heavier than any tiara I've ever worn, but I don't care. I feel weightless.

At the reception, we barely get to speak—well-wishers have come from all over the globe. I spy Heydar and Claudia dancing together and feel a spark of curiosity about the two of them—they would be very well suited!

As the night draws to a close, Santiago and I are alone, finally man and wife with the future before us—a future that I trust to be bright and long.

Seven years later

'Try not to fuss, little one.' I catch Santiago's eye and smile, before turning my attention back to five-year-old Clara.

'It's heavy,' she complains, lifting a hand to the delicate child's tiara.

'I know. I used to hate it too.' I wink.

'Then why did you wear it?'

'Because it's tradition,' I say. 'Tonight is a very special night and the people are excited to see you, their little Princesa.'

'And I'm excited too,' she says with a nod. 'But do I have to wear the tiara?'

Santiago settles Malthe, our four-year-old son, on the ground beside him, then crouches to Clara's height. 'How about we make a deal?' he suggests, and I smile, because Daddy always knows exactly what to say to win Clara over— just like her *mama*.

'What deal?' Clara asks, crossing her arms over her chest.

'You wear the tiara at first, just while we enter the room and photos are taken. Then you can take it off and pretend you are no longer a princess.'

Clara considers that. 'I like being a princess, just not wearing heavy things on my head.'

'Ah.' I nod wisely. 'Then let me tell you a little secret it took me far too long to learn…'

Santiago stands, putting his arm around me, drawing me close.

'What?' Clara prompts. Malthe watches us with interest.

'There is no one right way to be a princess,' I say firmly. 'Listen to your heart and all will be well, my darling.'

Clara considers that a moment, reminding me of her godfather Heydar. 'My heart is saying it doesn't like tiaras very much.'

I laugh softly.

'But I will do what Daddy suggested,' she

says on a dramatic, self-sacrificing sigh. 'Particularly if there's ice-cream at the end of it.'

'You drive a hard bargain,' Santiago observes, but he grins, reaching down and tousling Malthe's hair. 'But I concede. Ice-cream it is.'

Malthe claps his hands together with enthusiasm for this idea.

'Is the baby coming?' Clara asks, slipping her small gloved hand into mine as we approach the doors.

'Sofia is only two, way too young for a New Year's Eve ball.'

Clara assumes an expression of someone far older and wiser than her years. 'Yes, you're right. Let's leave the baby to sleep.'

I meet Santiago's eyes once more and we smile, contentment wrapping around us as we contemplate the family we have made, the love we share and the life we lead.

It turns out I was wrong. Happy endings aren't just for romance books and Hollywood movies after all. They're a part of everyday life and I am living proof of it.

* * * * *